A
SECRET
DECODED

LONAE ROLLINS

Cover Design
Joseph Rollins, Jr.

Interior Format and Design
DHBonner Virtual Solutions, LLC
www.dhbonner.net

ISBN: 978-1-7361879-0-6

Published in the United States of America

I dedicate this book to my son Micah.
"Progress isn't determined by the amount of time spent progressing
but the act itself of progression."
~ Jonae Rollins

CHAPTER 1

After gathering the daily mail, Zuri recognized the handwriting of the doctor, and her heart jumped into her throat. With shaky hands, she tore open the envelope and began to read...

Dear Ms. Valentine,

I write this letter to you with some urgency and a great amount of secrecy. Please understand that no one must know about the contents of this letter but you. I am honored to have been your doctor for all of these years. I also understand your need to have more children.

I am writing to you today to let you know that I can finally make that dream come true. Please contact me urgently, as I have great news.

Many ideas began buzzing around in Zuri's head. Urgency? Secrecy?

And then it hit her…could it be that he has found a baby for me?

* * *

"Come on darlings, it's time for bed. Time to turn off the television and go to sleep."

Elora Howard was talking to her four children, two boys and two girls, ranging in age from eight to fourteen years. Although she was trying to get them to retire for the night, the truth was that they were not going to sleep just yet.

It was a tradition in the Howard household that stories were told every night before bed, used by their mother to teach them life lessons. The children all congregated in their mother's room, where she read them stories from books and asked questions afterward. Tonight was no different.

The four of them walked upstairs to their mother's room, while she followed. Her husband, Ellsworth, was in the study. It was a sanctuary where he loved visiting and immersing himself in his work, especially at night.

Once the children were seated around their mother on the king-sized bed, Elora cleared her throat and started to read from the book in her hand.

"No, mère aimante. You've read us this book countless times," whined Mica, her youngest son.

"Have I now?" She smiled affectionately at him, her eyes twinkling. Indeed, she had read this particular book to them more than a few times, but that was because it had a lot of lessons in it and they seemed to enjoy it every time. Until now.

"Yes," he answered, smiling back at her.

"So, what should I read to you now?"

"Come up with a story from your imagination, mère aimante. An interesting story."

"I can't think of any story right now. Let me read you this one for the last time."

Oray, the youngest daughter, who had been quiet all the while, said, "Mama bear, please try. You can do it." Oray didn't talk much, but like her siblings, she was smart. She enjoyed the stories her mother would tell; she would stay engaged and eat up every word.

"All right, I'll tell you a story. Now, listen, everyone," she began. "A long time ago, in a city not too far from here, there lived a woman named Joy, who loved to help others and put a smile on their faces. Who she favored most were children. She followed her passion and became a teacher, to help children learn and teach them how to become responsible adults.

One winter, while school was on holiday, she went to the beach and met a young man who swept her off her feet. His

3

name was Philip. He was charming, intelligent, humble, and had a sense of humor. She spent the rest of the day sitting with him on the sand, talking. He told her that he was an architect who was taking a well-deserved long break. She told him of her love for teaching and making children happy. They discovered that they shared the same interests in books, food, and music. From that day, they became an item.

"Item? What's that, Mom?" asked Z'Haara, her eldest.

"Yes, Mama, what's an 'item'?" Mica asked.

"They became friends; close friends," Elora answered, then continued, "With time, she saw that he was attentive and romantic. He wrote her poems and slipped them into her bag whenever she came visiting. He made surprise visits to her class to give her gardenias, and sometimes, sunflowers. He created scavenger hunts for her because they both loved the outdoors.

"They dated for a while and it was blissful. One sunny afternoon at the park, while the trees were blooming, and birds were chirping, he got down on one knee and asked Joy to marry him. She was so overjoyed and said yes. Though she was quite young, it didn't matter, because her parents accepted Philip as part of their family. After their wedding, they moved in together as husband and wife. But they traveled around the world often, due to the nature of Philip's job. However, they both loved every minute of it.

"But then, Philip found a permanent job and settled

down. He built a big house and lived there with his Joy. In the fall, there is nothing more visually appealing than a deciduous forest and its vibrant, leaf-covered ground. Three years later, as the leaves fell and the air got cooler, Joy and Philip welcomed a beautiful, butterscotch-toned, cherry red-nosed baby girl with dark, curly hair.

"The baby was so beautiful and charming that her parents named her A'dore. A'dore grew up to be the apple of her parents' eyes. Joy did not have any more children, so A'dore was an only child. At a young age, A'dore became very fond of the outdoors and like her parents, she fell in love with everything that involved nature, from plants and animals to flowers and trees. You name it, she loved it!

"Her parents took her to a flower tunnel one year and it took her breath away. The tunnel consisted of more than one hundred flowering plants and had more than fifteen different collections of flowers. It was like walking down the sidewalk with rainbow-like arrangements of flowers hanging down from arches that surrounded them for at least a mile. The fresh, floral, sweet aroma that softly graced the nose filled her head as she walked through. The beautiful feeling was what made her admire nature.

"Soon, she was no longer a child. She grew into a kindhearted, cheerful, and adventurous young lady. After high school, she left home and decided to pursue a career as a paleontologist. This was all thanks to her parents' largesse (generosity). In the course of her work, she met the man that became her future husband."

"Mama?" It was her oldest son, Sebastian. "The story seems familiar," he said, sounding curious.

Elora laughed, as the children looked at her expectantly.

"No, darling. It is similar to mine, but it is about somebody else. It is fictitious, as all of your bedtime stories are. Can I continue?" she asked.

"Yes," they chorused.

"Okay. So, she met this young man named Josiah, who was also following his passion for paleontology, and with it, he wanted to travel the world and find out the unknown about life. Josiah was from a decent home. He had a strict upbringing by his loving parents, who, although they did not have much, tried their best—even if it meant that they had to borrow. Both of his parents were hardworking and never complained; at least, not in front of him.

"They spent a lot of time together as a family, bonding, and creating great memories. He was an only child like A'dore, but made many friends with all of the kids that lived near his family's house. He was taught to be kind, to share with others, and he learned to be sympathetic as well as empathetic. All of these qualities contributed to making him the confident yet humble man he became. The weather was changing, and the summer season rolled around. A'dore was offered an opportunity of a lifetime, to go and study paleontology in Australia until the fall.

"She announced the good news to her parents; they couldn't have been happier for her. They gave their blessing and told her to follow her dreams. Joy and Philip embraced her with love and engaged in laughter as they celebrated her accomplishment. She could wait no longer to tell Josiah, so she rushed over to his house to share the propitious news. He, too, was overjoyed, embracing and kissing her. He knew right then that she was the woman he wanted to spend the rest of his life with. She was kind, beautiful, driven, and intelligent. Who wouldn't want such a woman in their life?

"The day before she left was a bright, sunny day with a clear blue sky, the scent of lavender in the air. Josiah put on his best outfit, grabbed some change, and walked to the flower shop. He asked for a dozen long-stemmed red and white roses. As he walked to her house, his palms became sweaty; it was then that he realized he was getting nervous. To him, this was a special moment; he wanted it to be perfect, or as close to it as possible for her.

"Once Josiah arrived at A'dore's house, he stood for some minutes and inhaled deeply before mustering the courage to knock on the door. He finally did and minutes later, the door opened; she was standing in front of him with a smile on her face that reached from ear to ear, like a Cheshire cat. Her hair was pinned up and lined with flowers; she had curly pieces hanging down her face that swayed from side to side as the wind blew.

"Her parents peeked out the front door window to watch with interest. It seemed that they knew what was going on. And maybe they did, because Josiah got down on one knee; in that moment, in front of her awed, but not entirely surprised parents, he asked A'dore to marry him. A furiously blushing A'dore gladly accepted. Her parents were happy for their daughter. They were also glad that she made a good choice. Overjoyed, they congratulated the newly-engaged couple and invited Josiah to stay for dinner. Joy got into the kitchen and prepared a special treat to commemorate the day.

"Dinner was a pleasant affair. The parents asked questions and gave the soon-to-be-married couple some words of advice. A'dore and Josiah thanked them and promised to do their best. When dinner was over, A'dore helped her mother wash the dishes while the two men talked. Afterward, the young couple went outside to lie on the grass, spending the rest of the night under the stars.

"The next day, A'dore left for Australia. Though she was away from her love and her parents, she made sure to send letters regularly; they replied as well. Soon, it was time for her to return. Josiah waited in anticipation. Once she arrived, she went home, and then after some days with her parents, Joy and Philip, plans for her wedding began. It was a prodigious ceremony, which saw many people in attendance.

"After the wedding, she moved out of her parents' house and into Josiah's new house. Both of them worked together and at some point, their work took them to India. While they were on assignment there, A'dore broke the news to her husband . . . they were expecting a baby. Josiah was jubilant to learn that he and his wife were starting a family.

"His reaction was priceless. Josiah broke down and shed tears of joy. He grasped his wife passionately and they danced joyously. That night, Josiah took her to dinner and asked her to choose whatever she wanted to eat. He promised her that their lives would be more beautiful than that of Romeo and Juliet.

"Nine months later, their pretty pecan-complexioned baby girl was born. Like Joy said, when she and Philip got to see their granddaughter, she was as beautiful as A'dore was as a baby. They named her Raina; she was the delight in her parents' and her grandparents' lives. A'dore and Josiah went on to have two other children and lived happily ever after. The end. I hope you enjoyed the story."

When she finished her bedtime tale, Elora looked at her children, especially Mica, who usually fell asleep halfway into her bedtime stories. But surprisingly, all four of them were wide awake and very alert. They found this story very interesting. But then, that was not all there was to her stories. She always asked them what they learned from every story she told.

"Did you like the story?" she asked.

"Yes," they all chorused.

"Good. So, what did you learn from it?"

"That being kindhearted is a good thing," said Mica.

"Exactly, darling. Be kind to everyone, even strangers. Anyone else?"

"Being in love with the right person will make you happy. Like A'dore and Josiah in the story you just told us. And like you and Dad, too."

"Oh, Sebastian, thank you! That's right. Love someone whom you feel happy being yourself with. Who else? Girls?"

"Mama bear, I agree with them," ventured Z'Haara.

"Me too," quipped Oray.

"Smart girls. All right, that's it for tonight. Let's go kiss Pop and get you all into bed."

So, she took them to kiss their daddy goodnight, and to their rooms afterward. Sebastian shared a room with his brother Mica, while Z'Haara and Oray had a room to themselves. Despite the protests of the older two, Elora insisted that she'd always see them to their rooms and kiss them goodnight until they left the nest.

When she had seen that they were all in bed and had turned off the lights, Elora got into bed with a magazine and waited for her husband.

CHAPTER 2

*E*lora Howard, formerly Elora Valentine, was born to Mr. and Mrs. Sloan Valentine. They were originally from Canada, but moved to Paris, France. Her father, Sloan, was an architect, and one of the best in his day. He designed houses for rich and prominent people, and at one point, handled building contracts for the French government. At the peak of his career, he erected an awe-inspiring structure on land he had purchased and named it Harbor Estate.

Zuri, her mother, was a grade school teacher before her retirement. She met Sloan when he came to oversee a new classroom block that was being constructed at the school where she taught. One thing led to another and they began a relationship, which soon led to them walking down the aisle in the presence of family and friends.

Before he became a married man, Sloan was a small-time architect, but his luck changed when he married Zuri. He began to get contracts that took him to different parts of the country. The nature of his wife's job did not allow her to move around with him, but whenever she could, she traveled with her husband. They were so much in love with each other that they did not give thought to having children for three years. However, after a while, Zuri started yearning for a child of her own. They tried for two years; Zuri suffered four miscarriages.

"Zuri, dear . . . come here." He reached out his hand to grab her and pull her close. She sat on his lap. "I've got you," he said as he gently grabbed her face and then exchanged a kiss. He laid his head on her chest and sighed, "Ahhh."

"Are you okay?" She leaned back and looked at him cuppin his face in her hands.

"No, my dear. I'm not okay because you're not okay. The real question is how are you doing?"

Tears filled her eyes as she began to speak... "I'm not okay. I'm filled with rage, and pain and I hurt from head to toe all of the time. I'm in a precarious situation." She cleared her throat, "I just don't understand what's wrong me with. I'm a good person, I'm healthy and I would make a wonderful mother. What's wrong with me... tell me what we should do?" Sobbing profusely in his arms, Sloan holds her tight.

"First, I want you to know that you are an amazing person and nothing, and I mean nothing is wrong with you. Second, we just have to get through this pain and lean on each other for support. We can get through this!" They looked at each other in the eyes and leaned in for a passionate kiss. She wrapped her arms around him like she didn't want to let go. They sat holding onto each other for a while.

"I'm going to go lay down." He took her hand and walked with her upstairs to their room. Zuri squeezed the pillow and gently laid her head down. Sloan covered her with a blanket, stood up, and left the room. Once he closed the door, he leaned against it, tossed his head back and exhaled. He lowered his head and made his way to his office.

Those were trying times for the couple. At one point, Sloan suggested to his wife that they stop trying, as he was content with just her in his life. But Zuri, who had always loved children, refused to accept such a suggestion. Her perseverance and faith paid off because the fifth time she got pregnant, she carried it to term.

"I should make a special dinner and tell him the good news. What should I make? What should I wear? How should I tell him?" She bashfully laughed while talking to herself in the mirror. "I can't believe it's finally happened. I can't believe having faith works. I'm so nervous, anxious, and tingly. I'm uncontrollably happy and I don't want to contain it." Fixing her hair and straightening her dress, she headed to the kitchen.

"I can't believe it's six o'clock already. I'm going to

freshen up before my love gets home," she thought to herself.

Ten minutes later, the front door opened and Sloan walked into the kitchen where Zuri was setting the table. "Hi, my dear," he said, his dimples showing and his pearly whites shining. "Something sure smells good! What's for dinner?" he asked.

"Come sit, my love," Zuri replied, pulling out his chair and handing him a glass of sweet tea. "I wanted to talk to you. But first, how was your day?"

"Thank you, Zuri. Please, sit with me and let's talk. I'll get to my day. How was your day?"he asked, as he pulled out a chair for her to sit, while tapping the top and giving her a wink.

She grabbed the chair, sat down, and crossed her legs. "Dr. Eanoj stopped by today as a follow-up to my last appointment. He wanted to give me the results of my latest test. I guess he thought a house visit was needed. However, I'm extremely grateful for his unprompted visit because..." She walked over to the drawer, pulled out some papers and handed them to Sloan, "He wanted to give me this."

"What is it?" Reading and ruffling through the paper, he stopped at the last page and his mouth dropped open. "Am I reading that right? Is it true? Are we having a baby?"

"Yes," she responded. He jumped up from the table

and hugged her, lifting her so high her feet weren't touching the floor as he spun her around.

"I can't believe it. We're going to be parents... I'm so happy and I'm so proud of you! Thank you, my dear. The next six months will be a roller coaster of emotion for us, but I'm going to be ready," Sloan proclaimed.

* * *

Zuri was placed on bed rest by her doctor until it was time for her to go into labor. Days blurred into weeks and weeks blurred into months for the emotionally optimistic yet extremely enervated. On that triumphant day, after eight grueling hours of contractions, pain, and yelling, their baby girl entered the world, kicking and screaming. She was confirmed healthy by the doctors and after a few days, mother and daughter were discharged with a clean bill of health.

They named their daughter Elora; she was the sweetest thing that had happened in their marriage. Tears filled Zuri's eyes as she couldn't help but think this baby was her miracle child. She ignored all of the aches and pains of laboring to focus on the most important part of the experience . . . her daughter. She was beautiful, well-behaved, and intelligent. Her parents put her in the best schools and gave her everything she needed. Zuri and Sloan did not stop trying for more children, but their efforts were in vain.

While getting ready for bed, Sloan gripped the corners of the bathroom sink and mumbled to himself. Caught in the thought he was having, his mind drifted to his wife. He stood up straight, looked at himself in the mirror and said, "It's time". He approached his wife with the weight of the world on his shoulders and with that in mind he addressed his concerns.

"We have two choices. One may be easier than the other for different reasons, but we still need to choose," framed Sloan. "We can either put ourselves through the pain of trying to bear more children or we can appreciate the life we brought into this world and spend the best years of our lives as a family. You, me, and Elora."

"Sloan, I just… well, you know I want a bigger family; I'm so happy right now, but I want more children."

Continuing, Sloan said, "If we pick the first option, we have to wait and wonder if we are pregnant, then deal with the aftermath of emotion and mental distress of it not coming to fruition. If we pick the second option, we can be at peace with the situation and continue to live our days out as a small family of three; a happy and very fortunate family of three. I choose option two, if given a choice." He waited for her to respond, rubbing his temple and running his fingers through his hair.

Then, after a short pause, Sloan prevailed upon his wife to give up, saying that being Elora's father was a privilege and it was enough for him. He refused to consider an adoption either, so that was the end of it.

Meanwhile, Zuri was not the only person who wanted additions to her family. Elora wanted at least a sister and brother. She envied her friends when they told stories about their siblings and sometimes cried herself to sleep after playing with her neighbor during the day.

One day, when she asked her mother why she did not have a brother and sister like other children, her mother smiled slowly and said to her, "You are special and having you as a child is an equivalent to having seven children."

She did not understand what her mother meant then, but that was the only time she asked that question.

As she grew older, however, Elora got used to being an only child and stopped holding onto the hope that she would have a sibling. By the time she was in high school, Elora started showing great potential. She wanted to be an engineer and was working hard toward that desire, but that dream went with the wind in twelfth grade.

While in school she met a boy who piqued her interest early on. She focused on schoolwork, but he always popped into her mind. One sunny afternoon, she mustered up enough courage to start a conversation with him. Elora walked over to the bench that he was sitting on while he was reading a book of poetry.

"Did you know that Checkmate in Chess translates to 'The King is Dead?'" she uttered.

He smirked, "I did know that, but it's fascinating that you brought it up."

She smiled back at him with rosy cheeks, "Would you like some company?"

He moved his belongings from the bench and gestured for her to sit down. She fell in love with that boy. His name was Edward Blake and he played chess for his school team. He was tall and muscular, with infectious charisma and a full head of jet black hair. She was a library advisor and had caught his attention during a chess competition between her school team and that of his school. Although they couldn't be with each other day and night, they slipped love notes into each other's bags when they did get together. It made the cosmic pull they had with each other that much stronger.

My Dearest Elora,

The days that have passed since we spoke are piling up and my heart is heavy with a yearning for you. If only I could touch your cheek and see the love that shines from your eyes. I do see it there, you know. I do not doubt that you love me and that makes it all the more difficult not to hear you say it. "How do we get through this?" I ask myself as another day fades into darkness. How do I make it through the long night? And then morning arrives, and with it, only the dream of you.

Please love me forever.
Edward

Edward My Love,

I have read your note a thousand times. I want to bring the paper to my lips and consume it. That is how hungry I am for your lips....for your touch, for any news of where you are and if you are safe. If my heart could beat with any more love for you, I fear I would die. There are no moments that pass that I do not think of you. I am consumed with longing.

Please write soon!
E

My Sweet Sun & Moon,

Your note was a bright and shiny jewel arriving on a cold and blustery winter's eve. I had forgotten to check the mail after chopping wood all afternoon at the cabin and was thawing out when your face appeared, as if by a conjurer's trick. For a heart-stopping moment, I thought you had walked through the door. It was then that I remembered the mail I had picked up before leaving town. Can you imagine the joy that welled up in my heart when I found the small envelope bearing your handwriting? Thank you from the top and bottom of my soul, for you are my reason for every breath I take.

I am working on a plan for us to meet. Bear with me until I have it in place and please, please never falter in your love!

Yours,
Edward

They had a whirlwind romance which soon resulted in a Elora noticing some changes within her body. Elora was surprised by the news, but it felt so surreal to know that she was becoming a mother. She loved the idea of bringing a life into this world, but terrified for the unknown.

Senior year moved along rapidly—or so it felt for Elora—and before she knew it her life was forever about to change. She had conceived on their last night of high school, when she went out with him to celebrate; however, she did not know immediately, until she began to have a hankering for food every moment and noticed that her abdomen was getting rounder. Elora went for a test and confirmed her suspicion. The result threw her off balance; she was at her wits end. What would her father say? What was she going to do? She thought about getting rid of the pregnancy, but did not know how. Then, she braced up and broke the news to Edward.

Holding hands while walking along the shore she started rambling and spit out the news of her being pregnant. Surprisingly, he was ecstatic and looking forward to being a father. He promised to marry Elora once he had made some money and opted to go with her to tell her parents.

As the door opened, footsteps were heard in the kitchen. The smell of apple pie was in the air. Elora tilted her head back, closed her eyes, and smiled as she let out a sigh, "Ummm . . ."

"Sweetpea, is that you?"

"Yes, mama, it's me. Edward is with me. Come on and brace yourself." Elora lifted her eyebrows and winked at him. He returned a smile and squeezed her hand.

They walked into the kitchen; her parents beam with joy as they see their daughter. They exchanged hugs that lasted a second longer than the average hug.

"Come here, you . . . we missed you so much, my dear." He kissed her cheek.

"Ok, my turn... give me some love." Zuri leaned in for a kiss on each cheek.

"You too, Edward. It's good to see you, son." Sloan shook his hand and leaned in to hug him and pat his back.

"Mrs. Zuri... it's always nice to see you."

"Ok, Edward, my dear. We've missed you, too. How are your parents?"

"They're doing just fine, Mrs. Zuri. They said hello and send their best."

"Let's sit down and have some tea." Zuri went to the fridge and cabinet, to grab glasses and the fresh brewed sweet tea. "Mama, we have something we want to talk to you both about!"

"You do? Ok, what is it, dear?" Sloan looked over at Zuri as she gave a slight nod back to her husband before turning their attention back to the kids.

"Well, we wanted to tell you that..."

"We're having a baby!" Edward cut her off and blurted it out; then he looked at Elora, shrugged his shoulders, and apologized for cutting her off with the abrupt outburst.

Her parents took the news well. Sloan was disappointed, but there was nothing he could do. Zuri, on the other hand, was happy. If she couldn't have more children, at least she was having a grandchild soon.

The seasons changed and Zuri's belly grew nearing the final days of pregnancy.

Two months to her due date, Edward went mountain biking with his friends. They hit the trails in a pine forest on a mostly sunny day with a bit of an overcast. The trails were promising, and Edward was ready to hit the ground rolling. During the ride, the group came across muddy terrain, rocky debris, and a soothing river down below. The higher they tracked up the hill, the more intense the ride became. Once they reached the top of the hill, Edward felt a drop of water hit his hand as he shielded his eyes and looked up to the sky.

"Guys, do you smell that?" he asked, tilting his head back and taking in the aromas of nature. Lungs full of fresh air he exhaled and said, "We should get going. I think it's about to rain!"

"Yea, let's do it," replied the group of friends.

The sky turned dark and the clouds shifted from white to grey; the sound of thunder echoed through the forest. The rain started to fall harder, so they rode faster. Gripping his handles, Edward held on and stood up to pedal because the turns were so sharp, and the mud was so thick when they reached the halfway point down the hill. Taking the lead, Edward started descending the trail, but before he could see it, lightning struck a tree and a branch came tumbling down. Edward tried to steer clear of its landing, but in doing so, took his eyes off the path, thus falling to his demise.

While in the hospital for a checkup, Elora could hear voices outside of her room. On this particular day, she could hear her mother in the hallway speaking to someone.

"Mama, is that you?"

"Yes, baby. I know now's not a good time, but these men need to talk to you." She shifted her weight to the side so the men were now in Elora's view.

"Ok . . . do I know you?" She grabbed the bed handles and sat up slightly.

They proceeded to inch closer to her bed. "No, mama, you don't. I'm Officer Amari and this is Ranger Lowanna. We are sorry to bother you during this time, but we need to inform you…" his voice got scratchy and he became choked up. "Mrs. Blake . . ." Ranger Lowanna started to utter, only Elora was frozen, in shock. Her hands got sweaty and her body began to feel like she was going through cardiomyopathy. Elora realized it wasn't her pregnancy causing this reaction. 'If they're calling me Mrs. Blake, then this has to do with Edward. My love . . .' she thought to herself as she crossed her arms, grabbed her hospital gown, and buried her head in her arms.

"Are you alright?" officer Amari leaned in, asking.

Ranger Lawanna continued... "We need to tell you that there's been a horrible accident. We're so sorry to tell you that Edward Blake was found dead at the bottom of a cliff. While biking with his friends, the weather abruptly changed; with the conditions of the trails and his speed, he didn't make it down the hill. Again, we are so sorry for your loss! We can answer any questions you may have now, or after you've given birth, and had time to… to heal."

When Elora heard the horrible news, she grew silent, became dizzy, and passed out. Although she came to shortly after, the shock was too much, and as a result, she went into premature labor. Thankfully, her mother was by her side and offered to contact her doctor, Dr. Eanoj, at the hospital.

Elora had to undergo a Caesarean section because she kept slipping in and out of consciousness. The next thing she knew, Elora was looking up at bright lights from a hospital bed, with IVs strapped to her arms. Everything was hazy, and she didn't seem to have much feeling below her waist. There were doctors and nurses all around. They were frantically working, flittering around her . . . and then she heard the first cry of her baby.

Elora felt a strange relief along with the grief for her husband, and blacked out again—for how long she didn't know, because when she came to... she felt a strange pressure down there. The doctors were whispering, avoiding her eyes. Another doctor came into the room, and then Elora heard a loud gasp. '*What's wrong?*' she screamed in her head, but the words wouldn't come out, just a low mumble. She just wanted to hold her baby. And then she lost consciousness again.

Elora finally awoke with a clearer head and she turned to see her precious baby sleeping soundly beside her.

When she finally came out of her shock-induced unconsciousness, her mother was sitting on a chair next to her hospital bed, watching over her. She called for a doctor when she saw that her daughter was awake. He came in minutes later and explained the situation to her.

"How're you doing, Ms. Valentine?" He had taken the chart from the foot of her bed and was writing on it.

"Where's my baby?" she croaked.

Zuri went to the corner of the room where a rocking cot had been placed. Bending over it, she lifted something out and held it to her bosom, then approached the bed with it. When she got to her daughter's bedside, she placed the swaddled baby in her outstretched hands.

"It's a boy. He looks just like his father."

As Elora beheld her son, who she named Sebastian, tears started streaming down her face. They were tears of joy, both from having come through the procedure and for the newfound love in her heart, so deep, she could feel it throughout her body. They were bittersweet tears. She was happy to see the magic that she created with Edward, but sad that he would never know what his son looked like.

Elora spent two weeks in the hospital, being closely monitored before she was cleared to go home. Zuri prepared the house for her homecoming and took care of her and the baby until she got her strength back. With the calamitous news of her boyfriend, she almost lost the ambition and drive to be an engineer or anything else. She had been crushed. But her parents were very supportive. They stood by her, encouraged her, and helped her slowly recover. So she persevered; nothing was going to get in the way of her career. When she felt strong enough, she was admitted into a university to study paleontology. Her mother took care of Sebastian.

* * *

Months into her junior year, Elora met a man named Ellsworth Howard, also known as Eli. He was brown-haired, smooth chocolate skinned, lanky-figured nerd. But he was a handsome-looking nerd. He was in the final stages of his Master's degree in Paleontology and soon became her mentor. While working with her, he realized she was hurting and afraid to love again. She told him her story and even showed him Sebastian's pictures.

Though she did not know it, Ellsworth fell in love with her at that moment. Tenderly and attentively, he made her feel alive once again. It was not long before she began to feel butterflies in her belly, whenever she was around him. This time around, the romance was slow and exhilarating. They were married a few years after they met; Elora was the happiest woman on earth. She relocated with her husband to the United States, taking her son with her. Ellsworth fell in love with the child too, and soon signed the documents that legally allowed him to adopt Sebastian.

Two years later, Elora and Eli welcomed an alluring, espresso brown-skinned daughter they named Z'Haara because it meant 'beautiful flower'. By the time Z'Haara was a one-year-old, Elora was through with the university and already working. She enrolled her children in daycare and carried on with her job. Juggling work while being a wife and mother was not always easy, but she managed to pull it off well.

Mica came a year later, followed by Oray two years after. Elora's family was complete. She had two boys and two girls, so she and Eli decided that they did not want another addition to their family. Meanwhile, Zuri, her mother, had been acting somewhat peculiar since Elora got married. Looking back, Elora was almost certain that her mother's behavior started shortly after Sebastian's birth, only that it became more pronounced once she moved to the United States. Zuri hardly called, and when she did, Elora noticed that her mother sounded distrait. She asked her countless times if anything was wrong, but her mother said *no*.

During this time, her parents visited twice. The first time was a few months after they got married, and the second was when Z'Haara was born.

Then, her father died one night, in his sleep, at age seventy; her mother's behavior worsened. Elora and Eli went to the funeral with the children and noticed that Zuri was incredibly distant. Zuri blamed it on heartbreak, but refused to come and spend some time with them.

Picking up the phone, she called her mother . . . ring . . . ring. "Good afternoon, the Valentine residence, how may I help you?"

"Hello. It's Elora. How are you? I wanted to know if my mother is around. I'd like to speak with her."

Once Zuri came to the phone, she told Elora that she would prefer they exchanged letters instead of calls, as the static in the phone was beginning to make her hearing worse. A worried Elora told her husband what her mother had said; he calmed her down, attributing it to old age and advising her to do whatever her mother wanted.

That was how Elora and Zuri began exchanging letters. Communication became slower and less frequent, but since that was what her mother wanted, Elora resigned herself to obliging her. Lately, Zuri had been writing more letters, inquiring about her grandchildren and saying that she was hoping to see them soon. Elora and Eli began to look at the possibility of taking the children to spend the coming Christmas holiday with their grandmother.

CHAPTER 3

The Howard kids were divergent thinkers. Though siblings, each of them was different in a unique way. They had interests in different things and pursued those interests with passion and energy. Being anything but average comes with arguments, pettiness, and self-isolation. They were no exception to the rule, and because of that, they didn't always see eye-to-eye.

"Ok, kids, let's go outside and get some fresh air," Elora instructed.

"Come on you guys. Mama Bear is calling us," shouted Oray.

They all gathered outside on a blanket that was on the grass, surrounded by tiny daisies that shone as bright as the sun. "I was just thinking about how much I love you all and how much you've grown. I wanted to take some time to acknowledge some of the things that make you uniquely and individually special," explained Elora. "Ok, we will go one by one; I want you to name off a few things that describe who you are and what you've grown to become."

"I'll go first." Sebastian crossed his arms.

Z'Haara's eyes wide and lips turned, "How come he gets to go first? He always gets to go first."

"Yeah, sometimes it's not necessary to always be so prompt and proper, Sebastian," Mica said, jumping to his feet.

"Everyone, stop fighting. Let's start with the youngest to oldest," clapped Elora, as she looked past the kids to see her garden blossoming, the birds soaring through the sky, and butterflies flurrying about.

"That sounds like a great idea," smirked Oray. "I would describe myself," she started, as a smile came across her face while she contemplated what to say. "I'm considerate, regal, and affectionate."

"Is that so?" says Elora. "Can you explain why you chose those words specifically?"

"I'd be happy to, Mama. I'm now eight years old—well, almost nine, and even though I'm the youngest of all of my siblings, I try to carry myself like royalty. If I can, I try to never pass up an opportunity to help clean up or lend a hand whenever it's needed. I try to be aware of when I have the chance to do more to help others. I will add that I've never used or helped with vacuuming, as I'm too little to handle it properly."

They all chuckled while looking at each other.

"I'm also very versatile. I keep things clean, but during playtime, I do not mind getting dirty. I like playing with dolls, too… and caring for them. I mostly spend my time feeding, bathing, or having conversations with them. You all always look out for me and teach me new things, and I love you vehemently in return."

She was beautiful, like her siblings. Her skin was baby soft, better referred to as velvety, and the color of milk chocolate; a heritage from her father's grandmother who had Indian origins. She had curly brown hair and a cute upturned button nose. It did not matter that she was the youngest, but out of her three siblings, she was the most dominant and outgoing. She made friends with the kids who lived around their home, and they usually came over on play dates.

Elora smiled. "Thank you for sharing, Oray. Who's next?" She asked, waiting for Mica to respond.

"It's my turn." Mica exclaimed, jumping to his feet again. "As the second eldest son," he started… before being interrupted by Sebastian.

"Pfft . . . I wouldn't go as far as to say that."

"Sebastian, please don't interrupt your brother. You will have your turn. Please continue, Mica."

"I feel that I'm very fortunate. Having Sebastian as a big brother and role model made me a smart ten-year-old," he said, winking.

While Mica paused and mumbled what he was about

to say before saying it out loud, Elora thought to herself, 'he's full of energy, with a personality that anyone who comes around him couldn't forget. He always listened to his older siblings and was ever ready to learn from them. He wanted to be a good older brother to his baby sister and looked out for her when Sebastian was not around. I can't believe how much he's grown. His features are so dominant now. He had brown wavy hair, a fiery-gold luminance of dawn tone, and his hazel eyes made his freckled face stand out strikingly.

He was growing quickly and almost catching up with Sebastian in height, but he was still a child at heart. Mica liked learning new things and asking questions. He tired his siblings out, most of the time, with his never-ending questions, but because they loved him, they always indulged him, even after complaining. He was also outspoken and the first to report incidents to his parents whenever we came back from work.'

While listening to her sibling, Oray noticed a squirrel leaping from the branch and scurrying up a tree. While following it with her eyes, she watched as it weaved through a copse of fruit trees and jumped over a rose bush—the sky passing her in streaks of hues and silhouettes.

Once his thoughts were gathered, Mica continued, "I have a particular interest in watching birds, being in nature, and gardening. I'm a quiet gaper, who could move around trees and bushes without a sound. I'm also intuitive and can tell when anyone around me was moody or sad. One game that I love playing with my siblings is 'Hide and Seek', and I'm better than them at it." Looking over at Z'haara, he snickered.

"You sure are, love." Z'haara replied, grinning.

Reaching to stroke the back of his hair, Mica sat down.

"My sweet girl, you're up next," Elora said, rubbing Z'Haara's chin.

"Yes, mother . . . well . . ."

Z'Haara was the first child born to both Elora and Ellsworth. Petite and slim, she was a beauty to behold, with a glow that radiated her cinnamon hue. At just twelve years of age, she already knew how to behave and act, both at home and in public. Z'Haara looked like our mother, though people said that she was going to be a prettier version. Still, she never let her beauty get to her head or cause her to forget the values which her parents were always teaching them. Unlike many of her classmates who had raging hormones, as a result of just hitting puberty, Z'Haara was reserved. She knew that boys should be the last thing on the mind of any girl her age.

Sebastian watched his sister. 'Although several boys in school want to get close to her, my presence keeps them away,' he pondered before the sound of his sister's voice interrupted his thoughts.

"I would describe myself as hardworking, an achiever,

and an avid reader." Bashfully looking away, she mumbled, "I don't have dimples like Sebastian, but I have beautiful pearly white teeth and a bright smile that always lights up every room I entered." She smiled and showed more confidence in her stature. "My main interest is in books. I love anything that qualifies as literature, from my school books to newspapers, magazines, and novels. Since Dad gave me a journal, I've written down new words that I come across, with their meanings—building up and expanding my lexicon. I also love playing Scrabble and helping Dad cook whenever he enters the kitchen to whip up what he called 'special treats'."

"I'm not antisocial, but like to keep to myself most of the time, usually spending hours in the library at home, as you all know. I will say that my classmates tend to complain about my honest nature, but it never made me change. Even if I was going to be punished, I always told the truth. Despite my gentle nature, however, I'm very headstrong and witty, but those are part of the qualities which make me endearing, I think."

They all looked at each other cheerfully as she finished up her turn.

Looking at her daughter, Elora was thinking… 'Z'Haara loved the smell of library books. Smart, elegant, and charming, she had an eye for details and organization. As the eldest sister, she was gentle with her siblings and treated them more like I did, especially when I was at work. She could always be counted on to give sound advice, and she did not believe in judging anyone. Positivity was another strong attribute of hers, both with her peers and her siblings.'

"Finally, we have the firstborn!" proclaimed Elora.

"Sebastian!"

"Thanks, Mama. I'll keep my turn brief. Being the eldest of the siblings, I'd like to say that I'm a great big brother." He reached over to gently nudge Oray's knee. "But seriously, I would portray myself as athletic, a protector, and artsy. As far as sports, I love soccer, tennis, and basketball. I enjoy different forms of art, and even though I'm not an artist, I like to try my hand now and then. I have great sketches and silhouettes of people, landscapes, and scenic views, which I drew in my spare time. I pride myself on being somewhat intellectual and love playing chess, sometimes with our father, you guys, or friends. My friends are always there for me, and the few true friends that I have, I always try to look out for them.

Elora, daydreaming, thought 'Sebastian is the eldest. At fourteen, he was smarter than most others his age. He was sprouting like a tree, and muscles were already filling out his lanky frame. With butterscotch toned skin, curly black hair which reached his shoulders, and dimples inherited from his father, Sebastian was surely going to grow into a very handsome young man.'

Unplanned and unexpected, he was his mother's pride and joy. Sebastian was every younger sibling's dream. He was fiercely protective of his sisters and brother, especially in school. Once, a classmate of Mica's, who wouldn't stop bullying him, learned this the hard way. Sebastian left two palm imprints on his cheeks, with a stern warning to the whimpering boy to keep his distance from his younger brother. It worked because neither the bully nor anyone else bothered Mica again. The boys in school kept their distance from Z'Haara because they did not want to get in trouble with her brother, which suited her just fine.

Keeping his promise to keep things brief, Sebastian began doing foot tricks with a soccer ball that was nearby.

"Thank you, my dear. I hope this time together has helped you all learn more about each other, in hopes that it will bring you all closer in times that are challenging," Elora said. Then, tilting her head down, raising an eyebrow, and smiling, she uttered, "Hmm? Before you go, let's let in some love and light. Can we recite our self love affirmations?"

"Of course," they all shouted. Then, in unison: "I matter, I am intelligent, I am beautiful, I am proud of myself."

"I love you all so much . . . Okay, group hug." Huddling in for a hug, they all laughed and held each other tight.

"Ok, you're free to go! I love you, my darlings!"

"We love you, too, Mama!" they all chorused.

CHAPTER 4

It was a new month and the middle of the year. The time was four o'clock in the morning, and Elora's bedside lamp was switched on. She had awakened with a desire to respond to a letter from her mother. The last one she had written had been on New Year's Eve of the previous year, and she had just gotten a reply from Zuri the week before.

She knew that nothing had happened to her mother; however, even though the woman refused to talk on the phone anymore, Elora spoke with Mr. Dempsey, one of the staff at Harbor Estate, and told him to let her know if ever there was anything that went wrong with her mother. She had last spoken to him two months ago, and he had said that, although Zuri was acting more absent-minded recently, she was fine and kept to her appointments with her doctors.

Zuri was coming down with age-related illnesses, but so far, she had been managing her health quite well, or so Elora hoped. Her relationship with her mother was so strained that they couldn't talk to each other regularly. Since Zuri had rebuffed all attempts at mending their mother-daughter relationship, Elora had let things be. She was glad that she had a family of her own; a loving and understanding husband who was always there for her, and smart and interesting children who made her forget that she was an only child.

She got up and went to her dressing table, which had built-in drawers. From one of them, she brought out a plain sheet of paper and a pen, then sat down to write to her mother. Zuri had given the usual excuses for replying late and asked about her and the children. So, she proceeded to pen down a reply answering her question.

Dear Momma,

How are you doing? I just got your letter. I'm sorry about the flu that you're just recovering from. I hope you take your medications as you should!

The children are doing fine; excellent, in fact. They have been asking to see you. Ellsworth and I are looking at the possibility of coming with them to Paris to spend the Christmas holiday with you.

Sebastian is a big boy now. I have to insist before he allows me to tuck him in at night. Sometimes, I wish he'd stop growing for a while. I see him leaving home soon, and I dread that day. He looks so much like his father, it's uncanny. He's a great big brother, always looking out for his siblings.

Z'Haara is just like me, only she has a more beautiful heart. She's quickly learning how to be a lady, and as a mother, I couldn't be prouder. And like me, she loves reading.

Mica is growing to be like his father every day. Momma, he wants to be an engineer. Do you realize how happy that would make me? I couldn't do it, but I'm so glad that a son of mine wants to live that dream.

Oray is a baby no more. Before our eyes, she has morphed into a sweet young girl. She has everyone here wrapped around her little finger. And she's doing great in school.

Mom, you've got to have a closer relationship with your grandchildren. The pictures that you have of them are not enough. I might never find out what went wrong between us, but I'm still your daughter and I've not stopped loving you as my mother and first teacher. I hope to get a reply to this letter soon.

Please let me know if you want us to come this Christmas. We would be more than happy to spend it with you. And the kids would be ecstatic. What about your friend, Aunt Hanna? She is doing great, too, I hope? Tell her I said hello and I hope to see her soon. Ellsworth and the kids send their love.

I have attached the kids' most recent pictures, for you to see how they are growing. This photograph was taken last weekend when they went to the park.

I love you, Mom. I miss you, too. Please write back soon.

Love and light,
Elora.

When she was finished writing, Elora read the letter; seeing nothing else to add, folded it neatly into three, and put it in an envelope from the same drawer. Then, she sealed it and placed it on the dresser. She was going to post it on her way to work in the morning.

Her alarm beeped at 5:30 a.m. It was time to make breakfast, get the children ready for school and herself for work. The children made it easy for her. Once she woke them up and ran them a bath, they pretty much got dressed and sat down to breakfast, without her having to run after them as most mothers did. The parents and children had breakfast together before leaving the house at the same time.

The bus came every day for the children, while their parents each drove their respective cars to their workplace. They worked for the same firm, but Eli was Elora's superior at work. On her way to the office, Elora stopped by the post office and posted the letter. She fervently hoped that her mother would reply sooner than she was used to and that she would invite them to the Estate. She found it painfully hilarious that she had to ask for permission to visit her mother. She wondered if things would have gotten so bad if her father were still alive. Before his death, Zuri had been acting somewhat aloof, but after he died, things had only gotten worse.

There was an excavation going on at one of their recently earmarked sites, so she soon forgot about her worries, and instead, thought about the job at hand. The site was a proposed location for a big factory, but one of the architects had stumbled upon information that the ground held some fossils, so they got permission from the owners of the land to excavate their findings. They had only one week to do so; she hoped that it would be enough, and better still, that they would find something.

* * *

It was a Saturday, and the children had finished their chores, eaten breakfast, and done their homework. On weekends when they did not have much to do, Elora and Eli called their children to the living room and told them stories that had lessons attached to them. Using those lessons, they taught their children moral and ethical behavior and how to carry themselves in the world. They believed in the phrase, "catch them young". They knew that to give an individual a solid upbringing, training had to start from a young age, and what the teachers taught them would never be enough.

Today was one such day, and it was Eli's turn to tell them a story. "Children, are you ready?"

"Yes, Pop," they replied in anticipation. As their mother was "Mama bear", their father was "Pop".

"All right. Today's story begins. In a city not far from here, there lived a boy named Nick. Nick came from a privileged home, where he had everything he wanted. His parents were very wealthy, so they made sure that he lacked nothing. They enrolled him and his siblings into the best schools. Soon, Nick was at the university.

"At first, he was doing very well in school, but before long, he started hanging around bad friends. The reason he got close to these bad friends was that they seemed to be living a carefree life; as a privileged child, freedom appealed to him. So, he started skipping school and missing lectures to hang out with these new guys. They took him to questionable places, where they introduced him to addicting habits; such as narcotics and underage drinking."

"What are narcotics, Pop?"

"They are illegal substances that people take into their bodies, which can harm them. Most times, they can be fatal."

Elora added, "Any drug not prescribed by a doctor should not be taken. Do you understand?"

"Yes, Mama bear."

Ellsworth continued. "As a result of his new lifestyle, Nick's academic life became affected. His former close friend, Alex, whom he used to study with, called him aside several times and pleaded with him to change his lifestyle, as it was not a good one. But Nick refused to listen. Eventually, he completely stopped talking to Alex. Gradually, he stopped going to his classes, and soon, he forgot what his classmates looked like. He partied almost every day and soon became a drug addict. This means that he couldn't do without drugs. Then, somewhere along the line, they introduced him to burglary. Their targets were banks and big stores. Planning for each robbery took days, but they were always successful.

"It is said that every day is for the thief and one day is for the owners of the house. They went to rob a jewelry store one day, but something went wrong. One of the staff discreetly set off the alarm that was wired to ring at the police station. The police arrived within minutes. But Nick's accomplices were quick enough to escape before the cops surrounded the building. They drove away, leaving him behind. He was arrested and charged. The charges were armed robbery and possession of a deadly weapon. The court found him guilty and sentenced him to thirty years in prison.

"Alex came with Nick's parents to court on the day of his sentencing. He was now a medical doctor and engaged to a fellow doctor. When he told Nick, Nick broke down and wept like a baby. His mother wept for her son, too. She and his father provided everything money could buy for their son, but they did not pay attention to him, neither did they make time to teach him what he was supposed to know. So, they were all paying for it.

"Nick tearfully hugged his former friend, who had tears of his own. He said to him, 'Alex, I'm sorry. I made a terrible mistake, and now I'm paying with my youth. In retrospect, I should have listened to you. But I thought that I was having fun and living large. I did not lack anything, but I made the wrong choice. Now, see where it has landed me. If only I could turn back the hands of the clock. If only I could go back in time!' He turned to his parents and said, 'Mom, Dad, I know that you're disappointed in me and I regret putting you both through this pain. I didn't lack money. I had no reason to rob anyone, but I chose friends who filled my life with negativity. The only one to blame for my predicament is myself. I'm sorry.'

"And with this, he walked out to get onto the bus that was taking the prisoners to where they would serve out their sentences.

"That is how Nick ended up. He became a convicted criminal and lost his freedom. His friends who escaped were never caught, and none of them ever came to see him in prison. So, he was alone in there, without anyone who cared about him. The end."

Eli smiled at the children. "Now, it's question time. What did you learn from this story? Sebastian, go first."

"I learned that a bad friend could put people in trouble."

"Oh yes, they can. Z'Haara?"

"Parents should make time for their children."

"Correct. Mica, what did you learn?"

"I learned that we should not let people influence us."

"That's right. The wrong influence can put you in trouble. Oray? You learned something, right?"

"Yes, Pop." She gave him her adorable baby smile.

"Tell us, honey," Elora said to her.

"I learned that it is wrong to take drugs."

"Yes, darling," said Ellsworth. "Now, this story teaches us much. Upbringing matters a lot; that is why your Mom and I make time to be with you and teach you things you should know. If Nick's parents made time for him and taught him as we teach you all now, he would have known that freedom had its own time, and he wouldn't have gone after it prematurely.

"Choose your friends carefully. Bad friends corrupt good morals. Your Mom and I are teaching you that the right way to live is not a guarantee that you will turn out well. In the end, the best advice is the one *you* give yourselves. We can only do so much. So, the type of friends you keep is important. Do you understand?"

"Yes, Pop."

"Lastly, never be tempted to do drugs. No matter what anyone says, even if we're not there to advise you, say *no* to drugs. If Nick had refused to do drugs with his friends, he would have been in the right state of mind to retrace his footsteps when he started misbehaving. Honey, is there anything you want to add?" he said, looking at his wife.

"Yes, there is. Darlings, your Dad and I love you so much. We tell you these stories not just for entertainment, but as part of educating you. We are doing our best to provide for every one of you, and all we ask is that you study hard and be of good behavior wherever you are. We want you to make us proud. All right, my loves?"

"All right, Mama bear."

"Now, who wants some ice cream?"

They all screamed excitedly that they did, and minutes later, the whole family was sitting in front of the television with bowls of strawberry-flavored ice cream, watching a documentary on polar bears.

CHAPTER 5

A letter from Zuri arrived in the mailbox six weeks after her daughter mailed hers. Elora unlocked the mailbox that morning, and there it was, amidst the bills. She hurriedly took everything inside, dropping the latter on the center table, she sat down in the living room and tore the envelope open.

Unlike most of her mother's letters, this particular one wasn't lengthy, and she wondered why, before proceeding to read it. The letter was confusing and worrisome.

Dear daughter,

I know that you are deeply upset and probably disgusted by what I revealed in my last letter. My darling, I have regretted a lot of things in my life, but none compares to this. Love makes us do a lot of crazy things. I'm so sorry.

49

They say that when death draws near, and an individual's perspective changes, they think about righting a lot of wrongs. I don't know when death will come calling, but I can feel it in my bones. It will happen soon.

Please, I would like to see the children before I go. Come with them; they need to be here for this. I also want us to talk about all that happened and try to make you understand why I did what I did, though I know that this will be hard. I wish we could make up, at least for as long as I have left here on earth. Please, hurry up. I will always love you, no matter how you feel about all of this.

Love,
Your Momma

Elora was perplexed. Surprisingly, she wasn't exasperated. Slowly pacing, she thought, 'What was the 'this', Mama was talking about? What did she do that she was asking forgiveness for?' Elora was sure that whatever it was, it was the reason for her mother's behavior over the years. She cast her mind back to the past, trying to recall any incident that would have been responsible for what she just read, but she came up with nothing.

And what was it she said about the last letter? This was the only letter she received since she sent that last letter to her mother. The children never got the mail. If Ellsworth had gotten any letter meant for her, he would have told her, or did he forget? Or had Zuri written her a letter and forgotten to post it? Anything was possible, given her aged mind.

Well, she couldn't travel to Paris at the moment because of the job at the site, and the children were in school. She was going to discuss the letter with Ellsworth and see if they could visit Harbor Estate and spend the summer vacation there. Schools were vacating in three weeks, and by then, they would have been done with the excavation. Surely her mother could wait until then. She needed to know what her mother was talking about.

She thought about calling Mr. Sanders and asking him to give Zuri the phone, but she doubted she would get anything out of her that way, and then there was the matter of privacy. So, she was just going to write another letter to her Mom and wait until they met. But first, she had to ask Eli if he got any letter from her mother.

He was in bed, working on his laptop when she got back to their room.

"Darling?"

"Hmmm?" he answered, looking up.

"Did you get a letter from my Mom, from the mailbox?"

"Letter from your Mom? No. You always collect the mail, so why would you think so?"

"I was just wondering because I read her letter that arrived today. She said something about a previous letter apologizing for something she did, and she thinks that I got it, but I didn't. Here, read this," she said, giving him the missive.

Eli took it from her; there was silence for a few minutes while he read the contents. When he was done, his brows were furrowed in contemplation.

"What do you think she is talking about, Elora?"

"I don't know. I've thought about it too. Should we go visit her this summer?"

"Hmm... with the children?"

"Absolutely with the children. We could spend the summer there and allow the children to bond a little with their grandmother."

"I have no problem with you wanting to visit your Mom. I look forward to seeing you both becoming best friends once again. But then, we have to consider the children's wants. You know how much they want to go to Disneyland this summer. What are we going to do about that?"

Elora came to sit beside her husband. She held his hand in hers. "My darling, I did not forget that. And seeing that we have promised ourselves not to take their feelings for granted when it concerns them, we are going to ask them. Moreover, they have been to Disneyland several times. They have never been to their grandmother's. I'm sure that we'll be able to make them see reason. Okay?"

"All right. We'll talk to them later this evening. If they

do not agree with us, however, you would go alone, then they'll spend this Christmas holiday there. Sound good?"

"I have no problem with that. I'll just have to hope they all say yes. Fingers crossed."

"Well, since they had always wanted to meet her, I suppose they wouldn't be so sad about missing Disneyland this year. Plus, Disneyland is going nowhere. They can go next year."

"Yes. If I have to say that to convince them, I will."

They laughed at that and proceeded to talk about other things.

CHAPTER 6

*I*t did not take any convincing for the children to agree to go to Paris and see their grandmother. When they got back from school, had done their homework and had their naps, their parents called them together and asked them if they wanted to spend the summer vacation at Grandma's.

The four of them screamed 'yes'. Just to make sure, Elora asked, "Going to Paris to spend the summer with Grandma means no Disneyland until next summer. Does everyone agree?"

"Yes," they all answered.

"It's settled then," Ellsworth said, clapping his hands together. "We'll leave next month."

And that was the end of the discussion. The parents joked that unlike adults, people always knew where they stood with children. Their children were the best. They never made unreasonable requests, and always behaved themselves, both at home and outside.

The children were looking forward to the vacation which was in six days. They had already started making preparations for visiting their grandmother. Even Oray had thrown her clothes and toys into a bag. It did not matter that Elora was still going to do all of their packing for them. Their parents couldn't blame them; they were excited at the prospect of meeting their Grandma for the first time.

It was a weekend, so everyone was at home. Eli was watching the evening football match, with his wife snuggled on the couch next to him. The children were in their rooms doing whatever it was that kept them interested. The landline phone rang, and Elora got up to take it. She wondered who it was that was calling at that time.

Getting to where the device sat, she picked up the receiver and spoke into it. "Hello, the Howard residence. Whom am I speaking with?"

"Good evening, ma'am."

"Oh, Mr. Dempsey! Good evening. How is everything?" She could recognize his voice anywhere.

"Not good, ma'am. Unfortunately, I bear bad news. The dowager of Harbor Estate, your mother . . . has just passed on. She had a heart attack, and though she was given immediate medical attention, it did not work. Her doctor was called in, and he just confirmed her dead. I'm very sorry for your loss."

Pause.

"Ma'am, are you there?"

"Thank you, Mr. Dempsey. I'll get back to you."

With that, she gently placed the receiver back in its cradle, as Ellsworth asked, "Baby, who was that? I hope it's not the ad-selling people at this hour."

When he did not get any response, he took his eyes off his game and looked back to find his wife staring into space, her skin as pale as someone who has seen a ghost. He immediately jumped off the couch and ran to hold her.

"Baby, please talk to me. What is going on?"

"She's dead. My Mom is dead, Ellsworth." And with that, she broke into heart-wrenching sobs and collapsed against her husband. Elora was a strong woman, but the news was something she had always dreaded. She always feared her Mom dying before they made up, and that was exactly what happened. What hurt most was the fact that they were so close to making up and mending their relationship.

Eli walked with her to a couch and set her down on it, then sat beside her as she cried her heart out. He held her the entire time. He understood what his wife was going through, that she was not just grieving her mother's loss; she was also grieving the fact that they did not get a second chance. On the inside, he blamed his mother-in-law for putting his wife through such pain.

As he was lost in thought, she began to speak. Her voice was laced with sorrow, as she poured out her heart. "Mom was a good woman, but I don't know what went wrong in recent years. She let this happen. I reached out countless times to no avail. I practically became a stranger to my mother. Then, she finally grabbed the olive branch, and this happened. Why did she have to wait until she was dying, to ask to see the children? What am I going to tell them? How will they feel to have their hopes raised after many years, and then dashed just like that?

"And her last letter. I don't know and will *never* know what she was talking about. Why, Mom? Why did you choose *this* time to die?" She resumed her sobs again.

Eli held her for the next fifty minutes and reassured her in between her tears. He told her that she may have lost her mother, but he and the children would always be there for her. Soon, she wiped her tears and just rested her face against her husband's chest.

"Ellsworth?"

"Hmmm?"

"We're going to have to tell the children."

'Yes. We have to," he agreed.

This was another example of their unconventional methods of parenting—they hid nothing from the children, believing that being open with them would foster bonds that would endure until adulthood. So far, they were making progress because the children were never scared to talk about how they felt at any point.

"How are we going to tell them?" wondered Elora. "They'll be beyond devastated."

"That is to be expected, but we have to do what we have to do. They're children. They'll understand it in no time."

Elora sighed. The sadness of it all weakened her. "Shall we tell them now?"

"Yes, why not?" asked Ellsworth. "The earlier we tell them, the faster they'll come to terms with it."

"Okay then."

"Now, you be a good girl and wipe those tears, while I go get them." He kissed her on the forehead, before going upstairs.

Elora did as he said and pulled herself together. It would certainly not help matters if they saw her in a pitiable state.

Moments later, Ellsworth was downstairs, the children walking in front of him. They each took seats and waited for whatever it was that their parents wanted to say. Ellsworth sat down and took his wife's hand, and to her relief, spoke to the children.

"Children, Mom and I called you here because there's been a new development."

"Is our vacation in Paris canceled?" asked the ever-perspicacious Mica.

"Yes. More or less. Grandma has just passed. She died this evening."

Sebastian's mouth immediately hung open and formed a large "O" and Z'Haara gasped. Mica said "Noooo," while Oray burst into tears.

"I'm sorry, babies. I know how much you all wanted to see her. But this has happened, and we cannot change it," said their father.

"When is her funeral? At least we can go pay our last respects," Sebastian said.

"Funerals are not for children," Oray whispered.

"Oray is right. But she was your grandmother, so it wouldn't be out of place if you go. We'll see about that. Now, go back to your rooms. We'll talk later."

Ellsworth prayed that she and the children didn't become mired in melancholia. Still, the next few days were depressing for Elora. A lot of "what-ifs" ran through her mind, some of them so ridiculous that she began to question her sanity.

It was the third day after her mother's death when her lawyer called. He introduced himself as Anthony Roberts, Esquire, and asked if he was speaking with Zuri Valentine's daughter, Elora. Elora replied in the affirmative before he stated his reason for calling.

Zuri had written a will and made her funeral

arrangements with him before she died. She stated that she wanted to be buried, at most, two weeks after she passed, but that if her daughter was there before then, that the funeral should proceed. So, he asked when she planned to come over.

Elora told him that she had not decided with her husband, but that she was going to let him know when she did. Later on, when she discussed it with Ellsworth, they decided to travel a few days after the summer vacation. They were going to take the children with them and spend a couple of weeks there, before returning. Even if their grandmother was no longer here, they needed to see what their maternal home looked like and get a feel of it. Elora wondered what the content of the will was like. Not because she was money-hungry, but more out of curiosity. She had a good job, and her husband was a responsible man, so she lacked nothing. Well, she hoped that whatever the will stated was not going to be a problem.

The next few days were a frenzy of activity. The children had finished school, and as expected, did very well in their classes. Elora went to the market almost every day. She did not have any plans to go to the market there. She doubted she was going to step outside the estate gates except for the funeral, which she dreaded. Mr. Sanders had been pre-informed of their date of arrival, so their accommodation was taken care of.

Ellsworth booked their tickets and made the travel

arrangements. He also hired a car from one of the local rental companies. They were providing a car and a chauffeur, which was going to wait for them at the airport and transport them to the estate.

Then came the day when they would leave for Paris. They did not know it at the time, but that was the beginning of the chain of events that would change their lives forever. Ellsworth drove them in his car to the airport; he was going to leave it there until they returned to the States. He was a practical man who did things in ways that presented little or no stress. Meanwhile, it was the first time the Howard children were traveling by plane, and they were very excited. They chattered nonstop on the way to the airport and asked a lot of questions.

Oray wanted to know if the weather in Europe was cold. Mica asked his mother if the house there was as big as theirs. Sebastian and Z'Haara were no different. At one point, Elora turned to her children in the backseat and said, "Why don't you all wait and see for yourself? It's a short trip by air. Surely you can be patient for a few more hours."

She turned back to face the road, smiling in nostalgia. A couple of decades ago, she was their age and just as inquisitive, too. She remembered her father, God rest his soul, saying that she would have done well as a defense attorney. She missed him even more, especially at that moment, and wondered if the situation would have been different if he was alive. She was almost certain it would have been.

For all intents and purposes, she had no family anymore, apart from her husband and children, whom she was more than grateful for. She shuddered to think about how bleak and uninteresting life would have been without them. Sometimes she craved her space and thought about the time she had only herself to think about. But always, in the end, she would have it no other way.

Two hours later, their plane was taxiing down the runway and in minutes, ascended into the sky.

CHAPTER 7

The plane bearing the Howards landed at the Charles de Gaulle International Airport in Paris, France at exactly 2:15 p.m. the same day. They deplaned swiftly and found their way to the waiting area to find their chauffeur. They were able to identify who he was, a middle-aged man with a crew cut and a pleasant face, because he was holding a placard that read: Mrs. Elora Howard and Family. Ellsworth walked towards him, waving, with his family following behind him.

"Good day, Mr. Walter. I'm Ellsworth Howard and this is my family. I believe you're our chauffeur."

"Ah! Welcome to Paris, Mr. Howard. Yes, I am. Did you enjoy your flight?"

"Yes, we did. Thank you. Meet my wife, Elora, and our children."

"Welcome to Paris, Ma'am."

He shook her hand and said hello to the children, then beckoned them to follow him to where he had parked the car. It was a Toyota minivan, which they found very comfortable as they got in, especially after their long trip. Ellsworth, who sat with him in the front seat, gave directions. As they drove to the estate, Mr. Walter talked about the rich culture of his people and various interesting sights in his country; he was French and very proud of his heritage.

Meanwhile, the estate was located in the countryside, so gradually, the streets lined with houses of different sizes and shapes made way for pine trees and whispering willows. There was greenery everywhere and the surrounding areas looked so peaceful.

Mr. Walter joked about the wildlife in the countryside and mentioned how peaceful and unfettered they all must be. It was not long before they could see the roof of their destination. Mr. Walter stopped in front of the gate and honked his horn.

Harbor Estate was an intimidating property. The gate was big, black, and practically told outsiders to stay clear. Flanking it were statues of lions, the two of them on their hind legs, as though about to pounce. The estate fence was as high as the gate and electric barbed wires ran its entire length, as far as the eye could see. It was a residential fortress made of bricks.

Seconds later, the gate slid open to reveal one of the biggest and majestic houses the children had ever seen.

"Wow!" they exclaimed, awestruck. Even their chauffeur was very impressed. He drove into the compound, which had a long driveway. Tall willow trees were planted every few meters on both sides. The compound was very large. It could have easily taken five more houses of that size. There were two smaller bungalows several feet away and they were just as beautiful.

The uniformed gateman who let them in waved a greeting as he slid the gate closed at their entrance. Getting to the front of the house, uniformed people were standing and waiting for them; men, women, and children. A few of the adults and none of the children had uniforms on. Elora told the chauffeur where to park, and when he did, the doors were opened by the occupants of the car. One of the uniformed men came forward and bowed slightly before Elora. He was a tall and distinguished-looking man, with hair a salt and pepper color, likely in his late sixties.

"Welcome home, ma'am. We have been looking forward to your arrival."

"Mr. Dempsey. Thank you so much. I'm glad to be home. I wish the circumstances were different, though."

"My condolences once again, ma'am." Then, he turned to Ellsworth. "Welcome, sir. We are pleased to have you."

"Thank you, Mr. Dempsey. Thank you," Ellsworth said, patting the man's shoulder.

"And this must be Sebastian and his siblings." He welcomed them and let them introduce themselves, which they did politely. He told them that he was the butler and groundskeeper of Harbor Estate, and had been with the family since their mother was a little girl, which made Elora giggle girlishly. Then, he gesticulated to the other members of the staff to come forward and introduce themselves.

There was Mr. Sullivan, the gardener. He was a bit younger than Mr. Dempsey and bald. He lived in the staff quarters, one of the beautiful bungalows, with his wife Clara; an attractive woman in her forties who had a nice smile. Their two children, Cairo and Theo, were about fifteen and seventeen years, respectively. Then, there was the gateman who introduced himself as William. He was the youngest of all the men. He looked to be in his early thirties. His wife, Ella, came forward. She was a striking beauty, but didn't seem to be aware of her looks. She curtsied and introduced her only child, Hasina Celine.

Next was Marie Alexander. She was in her early thirties and very attractive. She was effusive in her greeting and hugged the children one after the other. Her mother used to be the cook, but died a few years ago, so Zuri took her under her wing. She had stayed ever since, becoming Mrs. Valentine's cook and the estate keeper. She had a room in the estate and oversaw the running of the large house.

The remaining two adults were elderly women, in

their late fifties or early sixties. They styled their hair in tight buns and both bore a stern demeanor. They were the estate children's governesses, in charge of etiquette and learning. One of them, Hanna, had been around since Elora was a teenager. She was her mother's friend and a retired high school teacher, who lost her husband early in her marriage and refused to get married again. So, the Valentines asked her to come and live with them.

Her husband had left her a sizable amount of money, so she stopped work, opting to be a homeschool teacher. They gave her a bungalow to herself, which she now shared with the other governess, Nora. Elora was privileged to be tutored by her for some years before she left for college. She was strict as she was understanding. Coming forward, she enveloped Elora in a tight embrace and began to sob softly while everyone else watched. Then, as abruptly as she had started sobbing, she stopped, stooped down, and spoke to the children, telling them to look forward to some lessons in etiquette for as long as they were to stay.

The children of the staff were homeschooled, she told the Howards, and they did better than their mates who went to conventional schools. Elora smiled and said that she looked forward to her children receiving some nice lessons from the women.

Finally, three children came forward. Marie Alexander introduced them as Seth, Lotus, and Nilah. They were less-privileged children whom Zuri had taken in and raised as hers. When everyone had been introduced, they welcomed the guests and commiserated with them.

After that, Elora addressed them. "I thank every one of you here. Thanks to you, this place has been running smoothly. My mother's death is a horrible loss, one that hit my family and me very hard. We believe that she's in a better place today. She was good to everyone and could never hurt a fly. I'm privileged to have been raised by her and I'm raising my children to be better. You all are highly appreciated. Thank you all, once again."

"Lunch is waiting, ma'am. We have prepared your rooms and run hot water for all of you to bathe." It was Marie speaking.

Then, Hanna fished out a key from her pocket. "Here's the key to your Mom's room. Nothing has been touched."

"Thank you, Aunt Hanna. You have been so kind. And thank you for being with Mom all these years. I'm sure that your friendship with her made her so happy." She took the key from her and kissed her cheek.

"Now, let's all go inside," she said, taking her two youngest by the hands and entering the home, as her husband and other children followed. The staff came behind, bearing their luggage.

She was once again in her father's house.

CHAPTER 8

I opened my eyes to the sunlight streaming through my window. The Howards are arriving today, and everything has been prepared in anticipation of their visit. Though the summer break has begun, there's nothing like that for me. I may not have any job outside here, but I work every day, and I love my job. Running and keeping this estate in good shape is no small responsibility. Being appreciated for my efforts gives me joy and that is more than enough, Marie Alexander thought to herself.

A few days ago, we were informed that Ms. Elora and her kids were arriving soon. I gathered all the workers in the house to have our morning meeting over a buffet-style breakfast and we spoke about the chores for the day, tasks for the week, and the upcoming funeral. Lady Zuri's death hit me hard and I'm yet to recover. She was a fine woman, and life wouldn't have been the same without her. She never discriminated and treated every one of the staff as members of her family. Love was spread daily and there was no form of intimidation from anyone.

I can still remember everything that was said during the meeting, word for word. I allow myself to have a flashback, just because I can.

The meeting started by 11 a.m., in the great dining room. By this time, chores had been done and the children had been given morning lessons. I let my mind wander to the meeting.

"Good morning everyone," began Mr. Dempsey. "We all know why we are gathered here today. Lady Zuri, God rest her soul, had a daughter, Elora. She called me two days ago. She arrives with her family the day after tomorrow. As the groundskeeper, it is my responsibility to see that everything is in great shape before they arrive. Though her children have never been here, thanks to the information furnished by the late Lady Zuri over the years, we know quite a bit about them—what they like, their favorite foods, and their interests. So, we are going to make sure that their needs are met, and they are made very comfortable once they arrive.

"Tasks have been assigned to everyone, to ensure that no mistakes are made. As we all know, Mrs. Elora does not live here, and as a result, we are not sure of what will happen to our jobs in these circumstances. Therefore, it is in all our interests to be on our best behavior for as long as they will be here. That's all I want to say. If anyone wants to add anything, they should please do so now."

William, the gatekeeper stood up. "Thanks, Mr. Dempsey. I was employed here after Mrs. Elora left. Is there anything, in particular, I have to know, regarding keeping the gate?"

The other members of the staff laughed.

"Please, we should not laugh at him. It does not hurt to ask questions. Mr. William, please carry on with your duties as you have always done."

There was nothing else to add regarding their responsibilities, except that everyone was admonished to be steadfast in their duties, and avoid anything that would call their competence into question. Mr. Sanders then spoke extensively about the Howard family. He read from a notebook and, when he was done, charged them to remember all that they had been told. The meeting ended with a brunch of toasted bread and oatmeal.

I learned as much as I can about the children. They would be given a tour of the house, on the day they arrived. I hope that they are well-behaved. Nothing annoys me as much as children who cannot behave themselves or do as they are told.

My hair needs to be washed. I must look my best

when we receive them. It is not news that appearances always matter. But first, I have to take a shower and see to it that the whole estate is in good shape. Being an estate keeper can be demanding, but I love being here.

CHAPTER 9

The funeral was held three days later. Zuri Valentine had asked to be buried on the estate grounds beside her husband when she died.

On the morning of the burial, everyone woke up in a somber mood, but no one became exasperated. No laughter or noise could be heard in the compound. The lawyer, Mr. Roberts, came up to the house. He was going to be present at the gravesite and read the will afterward.

At eight o'clock, Elora, Ellsworth, Hanna, and Mr. Dempsey went to the funeral parlor to bring the body home. They came back an hour later, with an ambulance bearing what remained of their matriarch. The priest was already waiting when they arrived, and the ceremony proceeded almost immediately. It was a closed-casket funeral, another of Zuri's requests. She didn't want everyone to see her in that state, and she had hoped that it would help her loved ones get closure faster.

At the grave, tears flowed continuously. It was a family affair, with just a few outsiders in attendance. The latter were very close friends of the family, the reason they were there. Zuri's daughter, Aunt Hanna, and a handful of other people read their tributes, and finally, once finished, Mrs. Zuri Valentine, wife, mother, grandmother and matriarch of Harbor Estate, was lowered into the ground. It was a finality that was hard for her grieving family, which included her staff, to grasp.

As the gravediggers went to work, filling up the hole, the priests and visitors left while the rest of the family, including the lawyer, retreated inside. Those who were required to be present at the reading of the will were Elora and her husband, Hanna, and Mr. Dempsey. The location was Sloan's study, behind closed doors.

When everyone had taken their seats, the lawyer placed his briefcase on the table and pulled out a small envelope from it, which was sealed with red wax. He handed it to Elora to confirm that the signature across the flap was her mother's. Elora replied that it was and handed it back. He looked at them and slightly shaking the letter, he said, "This is the last will of Mrs. Zuri Valentine. Any other one is null and void."

Then, with a paper cutter which he brought out from his bag, he tore open the envelope and began to read.

Dear family,

*If you are listening to this letter being read, then I have
passed on. I hope that my funeral went well. Wipe your
tears, darlings. I have lived a fulfilled life and I wouldn't
want you to mourn like people who have no hope.*

*Elora, my sweet, sweet girl. I'm so proud of the woman you
grew up to be. I am so sorry about everything and I suppose
that we resolved everything before I passed. If we did not,
please forgive me. I am leaving the estate in its entirety to
you. However, it was not your father's wish to have it sold.
That property was built with love and sweat and is,
therefore, a legacy. Please keep it so.*

*Another thing. Mr. Roberts will prepare the necessary
paperwork for what remained of my finances to be
transferred to you. Do whatever you will with it. Also, I
have put you in charge of the staff salaries and made you
the executor of the trust fund for all the children in the
estate. Take care, my daughter.*

*Ellsworth, thank you for being a great son-in-law. You are
the best I could ever ask for. I'm sorry that the same cannot
be said of me as a mother-in-law.*

Hanna, my best friend. Your friendship was one I would

*never have traded for anything. Thank you for supporting
me at all costs. The bungalow is yours, until the day you
breathe your last and that is final.*

*Mr. Dempsey, you were my right-hand man, from the day
you came knocking on the gate for a job. Your service is
eternally appreciated. Like my dearest friend, Hanna,
Harbor Estate is your home, until your demise or you say
otherwise.*

*I want you to always look out for each other, and not make
the kinds of silly mistakes I did. Hold your loved ones tight;
love them like it's your last day. May you all find peace and
the strength to move on after my death.*

*From your mother and friend,
Zuri Valentine*

By the time Mr. Roberts finished reading the will, the
women were sobbing silently. He stood up, and after
telling them that he'd be in touch with them to sign the
necessary paperwork, the lawyer showed himself out.

The four remaining occupants sat and pondered on
all that they had just heard. Hanna and Mr. Dempsey
stood up at the same time, leaving Elora and her husband
in the study. Ellsworth scooted closer to his wife and
wrapped his arm around her.

"I'll always be here, even when you don't need me. Your mom might be gone, but you are not alone. Never forget that."

"Thanks, darling. I love you."

"I love you too, babe. Let's go find something to eat."

CHAPTER 10

*I*t was another day of the children's etiquette class. They were sitting on benches under a cherry blossom tree in the big garden and the other governess, Nora, was standing in front of them. Her class comprised all the children in the estate, including Sebastian and his siblings.

"Good morning, children."

"Good morning, Ms. Nora."

"Today we're having a class in etiquette. During the summer vacation, we take nonacademic classes every Friday afternoon and on Sunday evenings. So, I'm going to teach you all 'etiquette'. Say 'etiquette'."

"Etiquette," they repeated.

"First of all, who knows what etiquette is?"

Two little hands went up. She pointed to one of the hands.

"Oray, let's hear it."

"Etiquette is the customary code of polite behavior in society, or among members of a particular profession or group."

"Exactly!" Nora said, her face beaming. "Where did you learn that?"

"I saw it in a fashion magazine."

"Good girl. You've heard her, children. Etiquette is a way people carry themselves in society, which sets them apart from animals. Now, there are different types of etiquette. There is telephone etiquette, business etiquette, bathroom etiquette, wedding etiquette, corporate etiquette, eating etiquette, meeting etiquette, and social etiquette. They are classified thus to tell you what to do in each setting. We are going to take them one after the other, over the weeks.

"This week, we will be talking about social etiquette. I love interactive classes, so I'll be asking lots of questions. If you want chocolate chip cookies when we're done, then you must pay attention. Let's go.

"It doesn't matter if you are beautiful like me (here the children giggled. She smiled and continued) or handsome like Mica. People do not care about how rich you are either, if you come across as rude, impolite, or annoying. Behavior like this shows that the individual was not raised or trained properly. Do you want that to be said of you?"

"No, Ms. Nora," they answered.

"Good. That is why I will be teaching you how to behave when you are around people or out in public. Now, who knows what the magic words are?"

This time around, more hands went up.

"Nilah, tell us one, while Theo will tell us the other."

The youngest girl stood up. She seemed shy, but very smart. Her voice was very soft and silky. "One of the magic words is 'please'."

"Good girl. Theo?"

"The other one is 'thank you'."

"Great, great. You all are smart children. So, let's write it down."

There was a whiteboard facing the children. She turned to it and wrote,

"Number one: learn to say 'please' and 'thank you.'" Then she faced them again. "Be that child who respects the privacy of others. Do not go searching through your Mom's bag without her permission. Do not touch something that does not belong to you, without asking first. When you want to ask for a favor, always say *please*. And when someone has done you a favor, appreciate them by saying *thank you*. When someone opens doors for you, thank them. When Miss Marie Alexander serves your food, say *thank you*. Good children say 'please' and 'thank you.'"

She turned again and wrote on the board. "Number two: never interrupt anyone during a conversation."

Then, facing them, she began to explain. This was

how she taught nonacademic classes. She wrote out the points, then explained orally.

"You might have something to contribute when you are talking with your classmates or friends. Wait until the person speaking has finished before saying whatever you want to say. It is rude to interrupt people."

"Number three: do not gossip about people. Gossiping is a very bad habit. If you have something to say about someone, or if they have wronged you, let them know. It is wrong to sit down and talk about someone else in their absence. Also know that when someone finds out that you have been talking about them, they might stop being friends with you. And those that gossip with you about other people, would also gossip with other people about you. Gossiping is not in a nice form."

"Number four: when outside your house, take note of how you behave. Inside your house, you can sing loudly or even play noisy games, but when you are in public, remember that you are not the only person there. Do not shout or scream in public. Do not litter on the ground. After eating candy or anything with a wrapper, wait until you get to the next waste bin to dispose of it. When you sit down with people to eat, do not chew noisily or with your mouth open, and it is bad to talk with food inside your mouth. Spitting on the ground is also wrong. Well-mannered kids do not engage in such behavior."

"Number five: give people your undivided attention

when they are talking to you. Only someone who is ill-bred does something else when someone is talking to them. During a discussion, it is not the right time to read a book or groom your nails. These things can wait until the person has finished what they want to say.

"Children, who knows what else you should not do in a social setting? Yes, Z'Haara."

"Listen more and talk less."

"Brilliant! That is why you have one mouth and two ears. Who else?"

Sebastian shot his hand up.

"All right, Sebastian, go ahead."

"Ms. Nora, I want to ask a question."

"Yes?"

"If everyone talks less and listens more, then who would be talking?"

The children burst into laughter and Nora couldn't help herself either. When she had made everyone keep quiet, she addressed the question.

"Good question, Sebastian. Nobody is saying that you should not talk, but do not dominate a conversation. When you talk for a while, you give the other person room to talk too, while you listen. Do you understand now?"

"Yes, Ms. Nora."

"Good. Children, any other questions?"

"No, Ms. Nora."

"In that case, we are done for today. Let's go inside and have some cookies, shall we?"

The children were all very happy to oblige. Ms. Nora shook her head wistfully as she watched them run into the house and said softly to herself, "I remember the joys of being a child.

CHAPTER 11

*I*t was a sunny afternoon. Mica, who had been indoors all day, grabbed his binoculars and went outside. Birds were chirping, and he wanted to watch them and probably see if he could discover a species he had not seen before. He was going to look at nature and admire the landscape through lenses. The binoculars were a birthday gift from his parents for his last birthday. So, he headed for the grounds, away from the house and towards the bungalows. He did not want anyone disturbing his favorite pastime. Moreover, since they arrived, he had never gone that far.

"I wonder how many species of plants I can find here. It's so much land, so I'm sure it would take weeks to explore. I do coin myself an adventurer," he giggled. "I wish my siblings were here so I could show them all the beauty that lays outside," he shrugged. Let today's adventure begin.

So, skipping over the mowed grass, he made his way to his destination. He went past the bungalows to a cluster of flowers in a big circle, with a space in the middle and a means of entry. There were sunflowers, roses, and hibiscus, and he knew them all. He put the binoculars to his face as he slowly walked forward, taking in everything including the insects that were feeding and flying over the flowers. Then, he walked into the space of flowers, and that was when he noticed a figure sitting on the grass. It was a girl and her head was bent as she studied a flower which she held in her hand.

"What is that . . . wait, not a what but a who." He took the binoculars away from his face and let it fall to hang on his neck as the figure looked up at him. It was Nilah, one of the estate children. She looked surprised to see him; he had not expected to see her or anyone else there, either.

"Hi," she said.

"Hi," he replied, then added, "I hope I'm not trespassing."

The girl laughed. It was like the clinking sound of glasses. Then, she said, "You are not trespassing. This is your home. Anyway, I love solitude and I usually come here to get that, whenever I'm done with my chores. You can come to sit down if you want."

Mica went closer and sat beside her. "I love watching

nature . . . that is why I came this far. Do you like nature, too?"

"Of course I do. I come here almost every day. Your binoculars are nice-looking. Can I look through them?"

"Sure. Here they are." He unslung them from his neck and gave them to her.

She put them to her face and smiled. "They make everything clearer. Watching nature would be fun for you, with them."

"Yes, it is. I got them on my last birthday from my parents."

"Wow! Lucky you. My parents are dead."

"Uh oh! I'm sorry to hear that."

"It's okay. It was a long time ago when I was little. Luckily, your grandmother took me in along with Lotus and Seth. We grew up together and are like siblings. But like all siblings, we have interests in different things. I love nature and puzzles, Lotus is a bookworm, and Seth— well, Seth is just laid back. I love them as though we were from the same parents."

"Oh! My brother Sebastian loves puzzles and chess too. Lotus is just like Z'Haara who is always reading a book. Since we arrived, I've seen her with two different novels. She and Lotus could pass as sisters, with their love for literature."

Nilah laughed again. "Well, reading is a good habit. It makes people very smart and full of knowledge. I wish I loved reading as much as I loved puzzles. But it's not such a horrible thing that I don't."

"No, it's not. In which of the bungalows do you stay?"

"The three of us stay with Aunt Hanna now. We used to stay in the house, but since your Grandma died, we've not slept there."

"Why?"

"I don't know. Aunt Hanna said that she wants to watch us for the meantime to make sure that we do not do anything stupid out of grief. But we're fine. She's just being paranoid for nothing. So, that's it."

"Adults always think that they know it all," Mica replied sagely. Even Nilah was impressed.

"For a boy so young you know a lot. That's good. So, how many flowers can you name?"

As Mica and his new friend were talking about nature, Z'Haara was in the Estate library, looking for a new book to start on. Walking past the window she thought to herself, 'Mica's outside again. I hope he finds something cool to write about.'

Her lips curled into a smile and as fast as she smiled is as fast as it faded. She had just finished the novel she had borrowed three days before and had thoroughly enjoyed it. During the tour of the house with Mr. Sanders, a day after they arrived, the imposing library was the only thing that impressed her. The next day, she found her way there and her grandparents' books had kept her fascinated since then. Inhaling, she exclaimed, "There's nothing like the smell of a book. I do enjoy being in a library and reading books; it's a happy place for me. I'm going to read today in a new favorite spot next to the window overlooking the garden."

The view, whenever she looked up from a book she was reading, soothed her soul. The books in the library dated back to the 1900s. There were several limited editions and classics. The books were arranged according to their types, for easy selection. These included historical literature, poems, novels, autobiographies, biography, motivational and inspirational books. Z'Haara loved all kinds of books, but her favorites were novels and historical books—after all, novels broadened her imagination and history because they taught her things about the past that she did not know before.

"Today, I'm looking for a novel. Since I just finished a book about the history of Paris and learned a lot about my heritage, I'm looking for something different." She had mentioned this to Oray on the way out the door heading to the library. "Finally, after a lot of browsing and reading the back jackets for overviews, I'm going to settle on one that I think will be interesting. The title was *The Godfather*, written by a man named Mario Puzo. It was a book about a Mafia warlord and promised to be an interesting read," she mumbled under her breath.

She took it to her favorite spot, where she had dragged a couch the day she chose the spot. When she got there, she saw a book on the couch. "What's this? I don't remember leaving out any books yesterday," she said, reaching for the book and looking over both her shoulders to see if anyone else was in the library with her. It was titled *Secrets Unraveled*. She thought it strange because she had not read the book yet, and even if she had, she always returned books to their shelves every day before leaving the library.

She picked the book up and studied it, to see if it was more interesting than the one she had already selected. She decided to go with "The Godfather", before going to replace the other one on the shelf. "You belong back on the shelf. Maybe a good read the next go round," she thought. As she attempted putting it back, the book slipped from her grasp and fell. She picked it up and a paper fell out from between the pages. "I hope I didn't tear the page when dropping the book. That would be awful and I would feel bad about committing a literary vandal," she told herself.

When it was in her hands, she saw that it was a folded note. The paper looked new and the creases were not sharp, a feature seen in papers that have been folded for a long time. Nothing was written on the back, so she unfolded it. There was a short note written inside and she read it out loud.

Hello, Z'Haara. To keep a real secret is to tell no one. To keep a secret that one knows makes it a story. Some stories are meant to be told and others are meant to be discovered. There is a secret story that lingers through this house. Find the clues and reveal the truth. The next clue is in a place where brains and STRATEGY are the only way to win.

Once she read the note, she turned it over, noticing there was something written on the back. The handwriting was faint and the words were tiny. It read: *Can you do me a favor? Meet me at the portrait that sits the highest in the house tomorrow at dawn!* 'A favor . . . first a clue to something that could very well be a game or a joke, and then a request for a favor. What is going on and what is it that is being asked of me?'

Z'Haara was confused. "Who would have written the note for me? And why was the word strategy in capital letters?" She knew her siblings' handwriting and this did not belong to any of them. She wondered who it could be. "Maybe there is the possibility that someone is playing a game with me." Distracted, she put the note in her pocket, while wondering if she should tell someone about the note or just ignore it. The house did not seem haunted, so that was the only secret to be bothered about. Making up her mind to forget about it, she decided to go and prepare a sandwich and pour a glass of milk for herself, before starting the new read.

In the kitchen, she made her meal, then sat down there to eat it. She had learned a long time ago that it was a bad habit to eat in the library, and though the one in question was a private library, she still stuck by that habit.

When she was done, she washed the plate and mug, then went back to her reading.

CHAPTER 12

*S*ebastian had just finished playing football with some of the staff and their children, had taken a shower and was sitting in the sunroom. Before him was cardboard and in his right hand was a charcoal pencil. He was drawing the cherry blossom tree that stood just before the garden—he had a great view from where he was sitting.

He had begun drawing at an early age, as young as five years. His mother once told him that he took after her architect father, who was gifted in drawing, too. Sebastian did not just draw; he recreated every line, every shape, and every image that he could see within view. Whenever he finished any drawing, the result always left him awed.

One day, he attempted to draw his grandfather, from a picture he saw of him. When he finished, he went to his mother and held the drawing up. "Look, Mom," he had said. "Do you think Grandpa would have loved this? We could frame it and send it to Grandma." His Mom had hugged him and replied, "My dear boy, this is beautiful. Grandpa would have loved it, and he would have loved you even more for thinking of him. You know what . . . let's frame it and hang it in your room. When you see Grandma, you will hand it to her yourself." It had been hanging in his room since then.

Soon, he finished the drawing, after which he cleaned up and folded the cardboard. It was time for chess. "I wish I had someone to play with. Where is Mica . . . wait, I think he's in the garden." Shaking his head, he murmured, "On the other hand, I do like playing by myself so I can continue to challenge myself to become better." He had been playing against himself for the past two weeks. He found a bigger and better-looking chess set in his grandfather's study and had been practicing with it since then. His goal was to become a very good chess player and compete against professional players one day.

Sebastian stood up and went to the table where he had left the chess set a day before. He had not bothered packing it up because he played every day. "Let's set up the board; I think, this time, I'll start with the side of the opponent, so I'll go second."

He started playing in earnest. Then, moving his queen to protect the king, Sebastian noticed a piece of paper placed underneath the piece. "How did this get there? How come I didn't notice this before? I've played more than a few games by now and I don't recall it being there." It was folded into a small square, which was why he did not notice it before he moved the piece. He carefully unfolded it and read the contents in a whisper to himself.

> There are two sides to the brain: the left is for
> logic and language, and the right is for expressive
> and creative tasks. You will need both to uncover
> the secret that whispers through these walls. To
> find your next clue, solve the riddle—you will have
> to come out of your comfort zone, and
> OBSERVE. United you stand, divided you fall.

Sebastian lifted the other pieces to check if there were more notes. There was no other one. He loved puzzles but did not understand this one. *"...You will have to come out of your comfort zone and OBSERVE."* He knew that the third sentence was the clue he needed, but again, there were a lot of things that he was not comfortable doing. The keyword was "observe". It meant that something had to be observed; in other words, looked at.

"But we look at almost *everything*," he muttered to himself. He hated not knowing things, and although he did not wonder who put the note under the piece, he was determined to solve the puzzle. However, after minutes of several failed attempts, he put it with the cardboard and continued his game. He was going to get back to it later.

CHAPTER 13

I have put out clues for the first two Howard kids. Two down, two more to go. I need to know who it is, and why this secret was so important to keep. But, how could she have concealed something like this, and kept it hidden for so long?

If I had not happened upon that journal, I'm sure that this secret would have died with her. It's a pity the journal did not specifically answer all of the questions I have. That is why the Howard children are going to help unravel the mystery. I have been observing them since they arrived. They are very intelligent and driven children, though they do not seem very close. Well, that is why I am leaving clues that would make them have to come together to solve the mystery. It is also for their good. They never got to see their grandparents and it would be very unfortunate if they miss out on knowing about this, too.

I would just have *shown* Ms. Elora the journal, but what if it backfires and she hates me for turning her life upside down? No, her children are best suited for bringing this secret to light. They have vocabulary lessons today. The next two clues I will keep until tomorrow when they will be free.

The children's vocabulary classes were taught by Hanna. She had a degree in the English Language, and that was the subject she taught before she had to resign. Hanna was glad that she still had the opportunity to teach because, like Nora, it was something she loved doing. She was a stricter version of Nora, but when she was not being strict, Hanna was a very pleasant woman.

She was with the children in the garden, where they had all of their classes. Already, some new words had been written on the whiteboard. She had written them while waiting for the children to settle down.

"Good day, children."

"Good day, Ms. Hanna."

"Today, we are going to be looking at another set of new words. As we have always done, you will give me the synonyms of these words on the board and will make a sentence with each one. There are ten new words for the ten of you. Each person will stand up, say a word, and make a sentence with the synonym. I will call on you according to your sitting arrangement. I will call out the words, call on each person, and they will supply the answers. Let me see those who studied what I asked you all, too. Are you ready?"

"Yes, Ms. Hanna."

"All right, let's go. Maya, the first word there is *pristine*. Go."

Maya gracefully stood up and with a calm voice, answered the question. "The synonym of pristine is 'pure'. An example is, 'She was putting on a pure white dress'."

"Great. Seth, it's your turn. The second word is *fatigued*. Give us a synonym and make a sentence with the word."

Seth was a quiet boy. Even during games, he hardly said a word. But he always had things going on inside his small head. Unless he was engaged in conversation, he never started one himself. He stood up and quietly said,

"The synonym of fatigued is 'tired'. Example: 'He was fatigued from the day's work'. "

"Excellent! Z'Haara, the next word is *considerate*."

"Considerate is a word that means 'to help'. Synonym; compassionate. Example: 'It is considerate to stand up for an elderly person to sit down'."

"Good, good. Hasina Celine, you're next. *Coaxed*."

"Synonym; forced. Example: 'She coaxed him to make dinner'."

"Wrong. Hasina, it seems that you have not been studying. I'll talk to you after class. Who knows the correct answer? Yes, Lotus?"

"Synonym of coaxed is 'persuaded'. Unlike the use of force where you have to make someone do something against their will, persuasion involves gently talking to someone, until they are willing to do something. An example is, 'His mother persuaded him to eat breakfast'."

"You are such a smart child, Lotus. Thank you. Oray, you're next. Synonym and example of *observe*."

"Okay. The synonym of observe is… erm... 'look'. For example, Mica always wants to observe flowers all day."

"*Not* all day," Mica objected while the other children laughed.

"Silence!" Ms. Hanna chided. "Nice one, Oray. Mica, you're next. The word is *defeated*."

"The synonym is 'overpowered'. An example is, 'I chased my enemies until I caught up with them. I did not stop until I overpowered them'."

The children were thrown into fits of laughter by the time he was done. Ms. Hanna was shaking her head.

"Mica, why does that sentence sound familiar?"

"I can't remember, Ma'am," replied Mica, smiling mischievously.

Hanna did not pursue the matter further. She told Mica to sit down and continued until the ten of them had gone through two words each, with their synonyms and examples. The other words included *adored*, to which

Theo gave 'worshipped' as its synonym, and his example was something about the Hindus who worshipped Buddha. Before long, it was time for lunch and the class had to be wrapped up for the day.

Ms. Hanna told them that the next class was going to be in a week and they should get prepared. Then, calling Hasina Celine aside, she wrote down a list of new words and asked the girl to study and memorize them in three days.

Lotus, Nilah, and Seth went with Ms. Hanna to her bungalow, while the other three children went in the opposite direction. Sebastian and his siblings walked a few paces and soon they were inside the dining room where dishes of food had been placed on the table. Lunch was a cheese and turkey wrap, one of their favorite meals.

Their mother asked how their classes had been going, and they told her as much as they could. Elora was glad about one thing—it was painful losing her Mom, but she was glad that the children were interacting and learning more about where she came from. She was sure that when summer came to an end and it was time to go back home, many things would have changed. What she couldn't have known was how her life was about to change forever.

CHAPTER 14

*S*itting down to watch nature with Nilah around was fun for Mica. She always knew what to say and was constantly telling interesting stories of her childhood. Mica was intrigued by her. He had never been so close to anyone before, not even his siblings. It did not matter that she was older than him by a few years. He just enjoyed hanging out with her. They had been coming to the spot where they both met for the first time, for the past ten days. Sometimes, they walked around and discussed flowers. She seemed to know everything about all of the trees and flowers. Mica had to get a notebook for note-taking whenever they were outside.

On this particular day, he couldn't find his book. He looked everywhere for it and even asked his siblings, but none of them had seen it. Then, he decided to go outside without it. He usually got to the meeting spot before Nilah, and he did not want today to be different.

Somewhat downcast, he made his way to the circle of flowers. When he got inside it, Nilah was not there, but the notebook which he had been searching for was lying on the grass. He was very sure that he left with it the day before. In fact, he made some new notes in it before going to bed the previous night. Still perplexed, he went and picked it up, flipping through the pages open to be sure that his eyes were not deceiving him. Yes, it was his book. But there was something else, written by someone just after his last entry.

Go look under the cherry blossom tree, beside the house. Keep your findings close for it may be a missing piece. You will need it soon.

Forgetting that he was supposed to wait for Nilah, Mica sprinted to the location where the note directed him to go. The childish impulse in him locked in. He didn't for a moment wonder if a trap was being set for him. At the foot of the tree, he saw a ribbon. It could have been white or cream, he couldn't tell. It was about thirteen inches in length and two inches in width. Across it, in block letters, was a single word, IDENTIFY.

He had been hoping for something exciting. A plain ribbon with a word on it was boring. But the instruction said to keep it, so that was exactly what he did. He tied it around his wrist and went back to his spot, hoping that Nilah wasn't there yet. She was not, and he sat down to wait for her.

She arrived almost immediately. She apologized for coming late, saying that she had to make lunch first as they all took turns every day, and it was her turn today. "All right, what have you been up to?" she asked. "Named any new flowers yet?"

"No. You're the one who does that best."

"You bet. Hey! What's that on your hand?"

"Oh! It's a ribbon."

"Why is it tied around your wrist?"

"I just felt like decorating my arm." For some reason, he decided not to tell her about his strange instruction. Maybe there was a reward for keeping to the instructions. He was sure that it was a secret game. He had heard a lot about games like that, where people score points for keeping to the rules.

"Funny thing to decorate your arm with. It looks so girly." She giggled.

"Yeah. It does. Let's talk nature," he suggested, smartly changing the subject. Nilah noticed, but did not push it. He was her only friend, and it would be foolish to push him away by her actions or words.

Soon the talk about ribbons was forgotten and replaced with a discussion about different species of birds.

Then, they moved over to debates about what animals were considered acceptable as pets and which ones were not. Mica said that the only animals which should be kept as pets were dogs, cats, and white rats.

Nilah disagreed with him. According to her, any animal could be domesticated, even lions and tigers. "They are natural hunters. I saw that on the Discovery Channel one day."

"Why would someone want to keep a lion or wild animal, for that matter?" Mica had a look of surprise on his face.

"To show off, I suppose. There is no other logical reason for that."

"I prefer seeing animals in their habitats. Whenever I watch them on the Discovery Channel, I feel like going into the television and watching them in real-time. Though I doubt that those who make the films stay close to the animal."

"I doubt they do. Maybe they use a helicopter or a car. But I'm almost certain that they do not go close to the animals."

"Or, maybe the animals are domesticated. You said so yourself," he joked.

"Hahaha! Silly boy. No, those are not."

Like other days, evening met them still talking. And they would still have kept on with their conversation if they hadn't noticed that it was getting dark and the adults might begin to get worried. So they bade each other adieu and promised to meet again the next day to pick up from where they had left off. With that, they both retired to their respective homes.

CHAPTER 15

*I*t is almost done. Mica has gotten his clue. It took a lot of thinking to come up with the idea of using a ribbon. I would just have given everything away. Actually, I almost did, but there's no fun in that. The purpose of drawing the suspense out like this is to learn how smart the children are and then, to bring them closer. Over the weeks, I have noticed that they all have varying interests that each of them pursued with enthusiasm.

As a result, they become so engrossed with what they love, they forget that family is the greatest gift. I wish *I* had the chance they are misusing right now. My life would have turned out better, I'm sure. But then, I'm way too old to be reminiscing about my childhood.

I cannot lie, I was *very* shocked by the contents of Lady Zuri's small journal. She was a good woman, but she did something that was horribly selfish. What was she *thinking*? And she went to her grave with knowledge as life-changing as this. It is so unfair, and I am not going to allow her secret to rob a family of the joy and opportunities they deserve.

Once again, I replay the way I felt as I read some of the entries in the journal, and I shudder involuntarily. Human beings are despicable. Beneath the nice and wonderful exterior usually lies something sinister. In the case of Lady Zuri, she was malevolent. Yes, because it is only a monster that would do what she did to someone she truly loves. I do not doubt in my mind that Lady Elora wouldn't have stepped foot here if she knew what her mother had done, and nobody would have blamed her. I guess it was fate that pushed me to pick up that journal. I was asked to clean the room without touching anything. But of course, my stubborn alter ego was having none of that.

For the hundredth time, I pick up the journal from underneath my bed, where I have been hiding it. If it is seen in my possession, I do not know what my punishment would be and I do *not* want to find out.

I first pull out the small picture in the middle of the journal. In the picture, Zuri is carrying a child in her arms. The baby does not look to be more than a few months. It is not Lady Elora, because the baby has a head full of hair; meanwhile, in the many baby pictures I have seen of Lady Elora, including the one hanging in the hall, she was bald. Lady Zuri is smiling down at the baby, who is facing the camera.

I put the picture back and flip through the pages, to the most implicating entry. This is the first of the lot in a web of lies, betrayal, and deceit. She wrote,

Dear Journal,

I've done something very horrible. I should feel like a monster, but strangely, I do not. Elora had flown the nest and I was very lonely. Sloan would hear nothing about adoption, saying that we already have many children running around the estate and that should suffice. So, when Elora gave birth, it was like an answer to my prayers.

Yes, I connived with the midwife and took one of the babies without her knowledge, but then, one baby is a handful for a single mother. Also, I'm technically the mother, since Elora is my daughter. God! Sloan would kill me if he finds out, but I've made plans with the midwife. Yes, I have paid her to take on this secret for a year, while I go visiting. Then, "Peach" would tell Louis that she adopted the baby since she had no child. I lied to Peach. She does not know that the baby I "adopted" is related to me. Maybe someday I will tell the truth, but right now, I have no such intentions.

Hopefully, I will be able to keep this secret for as long as I can. May God forgive me."

How on earth could a mother do this to someone she loves? Why did she not simply adopt and lie about the baby since her husband was against adoption? And who *was* this Peach, anyway? In all my years here, I have never heard her call anyone that—staff, or guest.

I'm sure that the child is on this estate because her next entry says so. The problem is that she never said who the child was. Well, she was always smart. She knew that there was a possibility of her secret book falling into the wrong hands and it was a good move for her, but not for the poor child who has been denied their mother for more than one decade. The next entry says:

Dear Journal,

A year flies by so quickly, doesn't it? I'm here again. This time around, I do not feel any guilt at all. Everyone deserves to be happy and I refuse to be an exception.

My baby is home. Everything went according to plan. I have spent a fortune to make the midwife keep her mouth shut. Peach would have made a good actress. Sloan believed her when she told him that she adopted a baby because she had never had one. Bless you much, dear friend.

I do not know what name would best suit this new bundle of blessings. I have picked out four names, but I need just one. Oh well, that could wait for now. My maternal

instincts have already started kicking in once again. Ah, the
joy of being a mother is second to none.

Closing the journal, I let different thoughts go through my mind. When I first came across the journal, I played a game with myself trying to figure out which of the children it talked about. I still strongly feel that it's one of the boys. He should be the same age with Sebastian, though, I don't know how old Sebastian is. But again, it may be one of the girls. Everyone knows that twins can be different sexes.

It's time to leave a clue for the last one, then see how things will go from there.

CHAPTER 16

"*L*ook, Z'Haara. See what I found."

Summer was almost coming to an end. The tree leaves had already started showing signs of turning their colors. It was a cool evening, and a gentle breeze was blowing. Z'Haara and her sister were in the room that they both shared.

Z'Haara was looking up some new words while Oray was about to play house with her dolls. This was before she found the picture that she now held towards her sister.

"Where did that come from?" Z'Haara asked.

"I just saw it in my dollhouse."

"Let me see."

Oray gave it to Z'Haara, who promptly turned it around. As she suspected, something was written on the back.

Here dwells the other one of the ORIGIN.
What's unknown must be uncovered.

She turned it to look at the picture. It was her grandmother sitting in the garden in the summer; she knew it was the summer because of the marigolds blossomed near a tree behind the bench. In the front of the picture was a child sitting on a handstitched blanket, holding an umbrella, with her back towards the person taking the picture. However, she initially thought the child could be her mother, although there was no evidence to tell her that the child was a girl. Z'Haara had seen enough of her mother's pictures to know what she had looked like as a baby.

Z'Haara closed the book she was reading and stood up. Fishing around in her bag, she found the note that had been left for her in the library. "Oray, come with me."

Pray followed and walked behind her older sister, as Z'Haara entered the boys' room. Sebastian and Mica were on their beds, solving a puzzle and studying a flower, respectively.

"Guys, something's up, I think. Did either of you get a note or anything that had a message or riddle written on it?"

Both of the boys stopped what they were doing to look at her. Then, Sebastian answered. "I found a folded note under one of my chess pieces. Let me get it." He stood up and went to the wardrobe where he began riffling among his clothes.

"Mica, what about you?" Z'Haara asked.

"I didn't get any note."

"What did you get?"

"Nothing."

"Mica, you couldn't have gotten nothing. We all got clues. I think someone wants to tell us something. And your clue could help us."

By this time, Sebastian had found his note. The three of them stood in front of Mica's bed as he glared at them defiantly for some seconds.

"Just because you all got a clue doesn't mean I did. Why won't you leave me alone; besides, I'm good at following instructions."

Sebastian sighed in frustration and Oray crossed her arms while she shook her head. Z'Haara knelt beside the bed and put her hand on Mica's knee. "I know you're good at following instructions and I'm not sure what you were told, but we need your help and its important that we all work together on this. I know we don't always see eye to eye and I know we need to have each other's back to figure out what's going on. Can you please help us?"

Nodding, Mica reached under his pillow and pulled out a ribbon.

"You got a ribbon?" Sebastian asked.

"Yeah. A note in my nature book told me to go under

the tree. I found it there. It says "identify", he said, shrugging.

"Please, can we see what the note in your nature book said?" Z'Haara asked.

When everything was brought forward, the children sat down right there on the carpet and tried to make meaning out of the clues. They agreed that someone was trying to tell them something, but they did not know what.

There were four words which they figured were the clues: observe, strategy, identify, and origin.

"This is the time to apply what we've been learning from our vocabulary classes," Sebastian told his siblings.

"Yeah," said Z'Haara. "Maybe if we know what the synonyms are, we would be able to solve this. I got 'observe'. The synonym is 'look'."

"I got 'strategy'; its synonym is 'plan'," Sebastian added. "Mica?"

"'Identify'; synonym is 'determine or pinpoint'."

"Okay, that should do. Oray, what about you?"

"'Origin'; synonym is 'connection or ancestry'."

"Hmm," said Sebastian, scratching his thick hair.

"Wait. Wait," interjected Z'Haara. "Origin can also mean *family*. Wow! Family! I hope this is not what I'm thinking it is. Where's that picture?"

She read aloud. "Here dwells the other one of the ORIGIN. What's unknown must be uncovered."

Mica gasped. "*What does it mean?*"

Sebastian and Z'Haara exchanged glances, while Oray looked at them in confusion. Z'Haara shook her head, saying, "It does not make sense. Mama bear would have told us if..." she stood up and paced back and forth. "But then, who *is* this in the picture?"

"Maybe it's Seth or Theo, or Maya or—"

"Oray, that's enough. We get your point," Sebastian cut her off, continuing, "Assuming this is not a prank, then the person who dropped these clues wants us to come together and make a plan, then look carefully, maybe at the picture because we have some relation to the child in the photo, hence the keywords."

"But what if it *was* real?" asked Mica. "Something tells me that this is not a prank. Maybe we should ask Mother who the child in the picture is. Grandma did not get to see me or Oray. Sebastian, I've seen your pictures as a little boy, this is not you. Z'Haara, you had no hair as a baby, but it could be you."

"It's not me," she countered. "I don't recall this memory or time spent with Grandma. Let's show Mama bear the picture."

"Mica, you can show her if you want to. Just bear in mind that your legendary intuition can be wrong sometimes, you know," Sebastian teased, and they all laughed.

"Well, it's been a while since we all came together to

do anything as siblings. We might as well play a game or two," Z'Haara suggested.

A game or two turned into several games, storytelling, and puzzles. The children felt closer than they had in a while, thanks to a creative prankster.

CHAPTER 17

There was chaos at Harbor Estate. Mica went ahead and showed his mother the picture, and the aftermath was not pleasant at all. Elora asked where he had gotten it and Mica told her the whole story, even adding that his intuition told him that he had another sibling.

Elora was enraged. Who was crazy enough to play such a nasty prank on her children? She would have shown it to Ellsworth, but he was not around. Two weeks after they came to Paris he got a contract back in the States, so he went home every two weeks to supervise the excavation that was going on. He was due to come back in the next week, but Elora couldn't wait that long. She was going to find out who the culprit was.

So, she called on Mr. Dempsey and asked him to gather every one of the staff, both adults and children in the main hall. In ten minutes, everyone was accounted for, including her children. She waited for them to be quiet, before getting straight to the point.

"Thank you all for coming on such short notice. I promise not to take up your time. Someone has been leaving notes for my kids, anonymously. I do not want to go through the painstaking and time-wasting task of fishing the person out. If you are the one, could you please step forward?"

There were low murmurs as the members of staff standing before her wondered what it was all about.

Then, they slowly made way as someone from the back came forward. The footsteps were drawing closer to the front of the room, when suddenly, they were stopped.

"Is no one going to come forward and take responsibility for their actions?" Elora sighed. "Well, if no one wants to come forward, there will be consequences for all those involved. I can't believe you would put my family through this mockery and other such skulduggery. In case you were not aware, someone has been leaving clues for my children to put together that leads them to believe there is a child that we have close relations with that I've never met! How dare you make such an accusation and then rope my kids into your theatrics. I will get to the bottom of this and I will make whoever did this pay for what you did to my family.

There were low murmurs as the staff questioned what

was done and who could be involved. The room grew silent.

"I must take care of the staff because they are my family so I need to do the right thing," murmured Hanna. "I can't believe how nervous I am. I'm sweating like I just ran a marathon." She came to stand in front of Elora, head bowed, hands clasped in front of her.

An incredulous gasp echoed through the room. The room split as people made room for the person who was walking with confidence and shame suddenly stepped forward. It can't be. Aunt Hanna?

"No… No… but you know…" as she starts to trail off her words.

"Why would you do such a thing?" Elora asked, while dismissing the others, except for her children. When the last person had left the hall, she turned to Hanna and began to shout at her.

"What sort of silly game are you playing with my children? How dare you suggest to them that they have another sibling? Do you know how psychologically damaging your actions are?"

"I'm sorry, ma'am. I—"

"Just *shut* it!" By this time, Elora was furious. "I do not want to hear a *word* from you. I have a good mind to send you packing this *very* instant, and I would be justified. What you did was awful and way beyond the boundaries of expensive jokes. I will wait until my husband returns before deciding what to do with you. Now, apologize to the children!"

By this time, tears were streaming down Hanna's face. She faced the children and in between sobs spoke to them.

"I'm so sorry, children. What happened was a very stupid mistake, and I apologize for all that you've been put through since being here."

"Now, get out!" ordered Elora.

Hanna burst into more tears as she ran through the door. Then Elora faced the children.

"Next time something like this happens, do not keep it to yourselves. Let me or your Dad know immediately. *Do you understand?*"

"Yes, Mom," they answered, their voices subdued. They had never seen their Mom that angry before.

"Good. Z'Haara, go to Nora's building. Tell her that I sent you. It's not a weekend or a Sunday, but I want her to give you kids a history lesson, starting in the next twenty minutes. You children must be kept productive. Now, you other three should go get ready and wait in the garden."

The children slowly walked out of the hall in a single file. They walked so quietly that a pin drop would have been heard in the hall.

Elora sighed in frustration as she watched them leave. She wondered why they believed such a tale in the first place. She had been pregnant only four times, and that was that. She stood up and went up the stairs to her room. But with each step she took, she wondered if there was more to Hanna's actions that met the eye. Once she was in her room, she lied down and tried to calm herself. A few minutes later, she heard a knock on the door. It was Mr. Dempsey handing her a letter.

"Thank you, Mr. Dempsey. I apologize for my temperament earlier; this situation has taken a toll on me."

"No need to apologize ma'am. You've been through a lot lately." He uttered. "You should know that Hanna was just trying to protect her family. She isn't the one that left the clues for the children."

"What?!" Elora replied, slowly sitting up and staring Mr. Dempsey in the eye. "How do you know that?"

"Well, ma'am, I overheard your clamoring conversation with Mica before we all met and one thing stuck out to me. The day he mentioned he received his clue, Hanna was with me most of the day. We needed to go into town for a few items, so you see, she wasn't home to be able to leave a clue for Mica."

"Why would she be dishonest? Why not confront the person that did it if she knew who it was? Wait . . . maybe she was trying to tell me this, but I cut her off. This is just a huge mess and I still don't know who hid the clues for my children. I was so rude to her, but I'm just heartbroken about my mother and confused about the actions of someone still unknown that would conjure up this idea as a joke." Her cheeks reddened and her eyes filled with water.

"I'll bring you some tea and that should help."

"Thank you for all that you do, Mr. Dempsey!" Elora replied, teary-eyed.

Elora then grabbed the letter she had set on the bed and began to read the front. It had a return to sender label on it and she realized it was from her mother. At that moment, she realized "This is the letter Mom was talking about; this is the letter I've been searching for." Without hesitation, she ripped the side of the envelope and pulled out the letter.

As she began to read it, her eyes grew wider the more she read. She couldn't contain her emotions and let out a huge sigh followed by a scream. Her hands started trembling and teardrops fell on the letter. She looked away and immediately returned to continue reading the letter. Before she could finish it, she looked to see Ellsworth walking through the bedroom door. Elora looked at him so intensely that he promptly stopped moving; his face was now filled with worry.

"Elora, dear, what's the matter?" he called out.

"I… I… She... I can't believe she…" Elora stuttered.

She looked out at Ellsworth, her eyes filled with tears and her head spinning. Her vision began to fade, and she dropped the letter as she closed her eyes and fell to the floor. Ellsworth ran to her side and caught her head before she fell. Holding her in his arms trying to wake her,

Ellsworth looked down to see the letter from her mother and all he could catch from it was:

> "My daughter, you always knew I wanted another child. I just didn't realize that you would be the mother of that child..."

Made in the USA
Middletown, DE
19 April 2021